mushroom.man

For my friends
VERÆ AMICITIÆ SEMPITERNÆ SUNT.
—Marcus Tullius Cicero

mushroom.man

Paolo Tullio

THE LILLIPUT PRESS
DUBLIN

First published 1998 by
THE LILLIPUT PRESS LTD
62-63 Sitric Road, Arbour Hill,
Dublin 7, Ireland.
e-mail: lilliput@indigo.ie
http://indigo.ie/~lilliput

A CIP record for this
title is available from
The British Library.

ISBN 1 901866 09 2

*The Lilliput Press receives financial assistance from
An Chomhairle Ealaíon/The Arts Council of Ireland.*

Set in Cochin and Bembo Italic with Ergoe Regular display heads
Printed in Ireland
by ßetaprint of Clonshaugh, Dublin

mushroom.man

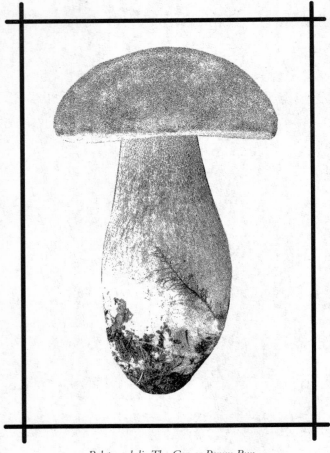

Boletus edulis. The Cep or Penny Bun.
Large, 3-10 inches diameter.
Brown-capped mushroom, white stem.
Grows under oak and beech. Early to late autumn.
Considered one of the best edible fungi.

one

You hear no crackle, no brittle sounds from the damp leaf litter on the floor of the oak wood. A dull, oppressive sky sheds only a limp light through the thinning canopy of trees. I move through the forest slowly, eyes down, straining to pick out the brown of the fungus cap from the russet background. Penny Buns: a well-baked bun of a mushroom with an ability to hide, to go unobserved on the first pass of the eye. You have to surprise them; spot them when they think that you've moved on, when they drop their cloak of invisibility. Not plants – beasts. To a zoologist they're closer to animals than plants. To me, too. Strange creatures that give up their secrets reluctantly. Clever. Not like a potato that any idiot can grow, or a cabbage, not easy to domesticate, not happy to take man's shilling: ceps will succumb only to the hunter, the forager, the man who knows the woods. I move through the trees. Beech and oak, an odd holly. The river roars in autumn spate below me. A jay chatters.

How old are these creatures? How long in the subsoil? Spreading their strands of mycelium, growing slowly, fruiting, eating, symbiotic with the trees. As old as the forest, as old as the land. A primal life form, complex, abundant, earthborne, airborne, maybe waterborne. A flash of red – fly agaric – the Norseman's soma, there under the big birch. Slugs feast on it: it's old, maybe a week old, big chunks are gone from the stem, the cap. There will be others around. The walking gets harder, brambles knit a mat that catches the legs, determined to snare the unwary foot.

Perhaps hiding in here, away from the deer tracks. I beat the brambles with my stick and feel better. They're aggressive; they fight back. Small, useless mushrooms are in here. Frail caps, frail stems, no taste, no use. I look up. Maybe a bracket fungus on a trunk? Not even that. I slash my way out of the bramble patch and walk more easily. Autumns in my woods are damp affairs; not here the crisp dry leaves of a New England fall. Just a mat of damp on its way to becoming leaf mould. And the fungal world works there too, living on the planet's underbelly, finding its niche in the rot and decay, in the dark and in the damp. It likes the humid, the fetid – there's no mould where the sun shines. But then, field mushrooms live in the open, they're the ones you can domesticate, the unsubtle ones that any fool can find, upright and white in a field of green grass. No mystery, no secrets, no taste. My prey is not like that. No, my prey is cunning, camouflaged and covert. Sometimes crouching in long grass, sometimes its brown cap lost in the dead leaves on the forest floor. My eye is trained to these woods, to my quarry. I think back. Rain four days ago, sun yesterday, is that the formula? They like some light, but not too much. They like it moist, but not too wet. They like warmth, but not too hot. Fussy little buggers.

Moving uphill. The trees are farther apart, the light is better. The deer tracks begin to look like forest highways, wide and covered in deer shit. You never see them in the woods – hardly ever. Just the evidence, just the marks they leave behind. The oak and beech give way to birch. Young, skinny things like gangly adolescents. Still no prey, but something nearly as good. Orange birch boletus in clumps of two and three, a bit big, a bit too mature and spongy, but good enough. Into the basket, wipe the knife, walk on. Badger set. Busy little brocks have left yesterday's litter outside the front door. I remember my last dog, a yellow Labrador bitch, beautiful and very large, who used to enjoy a quick roll in badger shit and then try to be friendly.

There's a clearing beyond the set where a fallen tree makes a seat. I sit; a gentle mist is falling as I look around me. All the leaves are brown, and the sky is grey. I sing it. Maybe a day like today. No, they have dry leaves in California, ones that blow in the breeze; you'd need a hurricane to shift this lot. Stuck together with slugs and wet stuff. I can smell mushrooms. The smell of fungus and damp earth, the truffle smell but less intense. I can smell my prey, perhaps near here. I stay sat, savouring the scent of the prey – is that a spoor? I'll look it up later. I can smell them. They're near. I lean back on the trunk. I stare at the watery sky. I'm a fool: of course I can smell them, they're in the basket at my feet. I sit up and check that's what I'm smelling. I lie back again. It is.

It's a hunt. It has all the feel of a hunt, the rise in adrenaline, the senses on red alert. I like hunting small game. Rabbits, pigeon, pheasant, mushrooms. You have to know your quarry, where it lives, how it lives. The more you know the more you catch. You have to get into its skin, react like it, you have to know its likes and dislikes, where it feeds, where it lives. The odd thing is that to catch it you must also love it. Eat it and it's a part of you. I never catch what I don't eat, not even a mushroom.

The light falling mist has wet me. My face is wet, tiny rivulets form on my coat running down to that huge sponge of a forest floor. I wonder how long it takes for the water to seep through the hill and come out in the river below. A week? A year? I decide most of it probably never gets there, it goes straight back into the air as tree sweat. No, not in winter – there are no leaves to sweat. They're like me, they only sweat in the summer. I sit up. Water runs down my neck. I pick up the basket and move on.

I have a plan. I am walking the woods in a big circle. I want to end up where I started. 'And the end of all our wanderings will be to return to the place from where we started and know it for the first time.' I seem to have found my starting-point as often as I've started out but I feel no wiser, just better informed. I'll walk the ridge, then go downhill to the river, then along the banks to the bridge. I knew this river before I knew it was this river.

In my early twenties, I think, I ate some peyote buttons and drove down here. I walked this river and hallucinated. Odd things happened. I walked towards a bridge knowing that if I looked over the parapet at the other side I would see two trout basking near the surface. And it happened just like that. Time twisted and warped and strangely no insect tried to bite me. Nearly six years later I moved to the river from the city. I had never been sure where I had been that day. A year or so after moving I was exploring the river downstream and I found the place. There was the bridge, the track, the view of the mountains. Here I first stepped into that different world. I found the place from where I had started, but still I only knew it to see. At least I know the river now.

I know it well. It visited me in my home late one August night. It came lapping at the front door, and finally pushed its way in like an unwelcome guest, until at waist height it started its slow, unwilling return to its bed, leaving its marks and tracks all over the house.

It rearranged my land, took away my drive, left a sandy beach where once there had been a riverbank, took away some of my trees and dumped others in their place, left two drowned sheep high in the branches like strange, woolly nesting birds. Yes, I know it well. I've seen it as a tiny trickle with pools of gasping trout, seen it as a lake that filled the valley full of floating artefacts never designed for a watery life. I've harnessed little bits of it for a water-wheel. Maybe it doesn't like being harnessed, like a pony I used to put to the trap. I know my river, flowing like an artery through my valley. I know my river, its shallows, its quiet depths.

I like it outside. Get wet, get scratched, get tired, get cold; be alive. Even being flooded has its virtues: you're in touch with the cutting edge of nature. It's not much fun to live through, but at least I've experienced it. I wasn't in cosy sub-urbia watching it all on telly.

From the ridge you can see the sea if you look east. It's about ten miles away, but today it's not on view. You can see cloud hugging the hills, hugging the coast possessively like a jealous lover. Some trees here have been hit by honey fun-gus. I eat this fungus, but today it's not for me. I walk past this easy catch and start downhill. There are boggy bits here, ripe with fetid black water, flatulent if you walk on them. If you can be bothered to look there are small honeydews growing here that catch and feed on the tiny flies. It means getting your nose close to the ground to see them – close to the smelly water. I only did it once; I don't do it any more.

There's been a lot of felling here. A swathe of Monterey pine has gone. Fit for nothing, Monterey. Too wet for build-ing-timber, too knotty for its own good, it doesn't even burn. Just goes black and exudes sticky resin. There are acres of this all around. It's hard to walk through a plantation of these trees; their lower branches lose their needles but hang in there, springy and irritating, always looking for a chance to put your eye out. They're better off cut down. Maybe they'll put in something a little nicer this time. Some native broadleaf, maybe. It's hard to walk through the remains of it as well. All the brashings have been left on the ground, they're still springy and irritating, and long grass has grown through and around them making them hard to see, easy to trip over. Only the bark has begun to rot, so if you stand on a branch on the ground the bark slips off as easy as a banana skin, while the spiky bits wait to break your fall. It's always a bloody fight. It's a malevolent universe out there, where an unguarded step can land you in trouble. Watch your step. Mind your head. Look before you leap.

I clear the clearing without a fall. A clear round. I'm on a track now which leads slowly down to the river. A good track; I can look around me instead of at my feet. Piles of

Monterey logs cut to ten-foot lengths are stacked at the side of the track. Bound for Scandinavia to become wood pulp or chipboard. I've been told it's not even much good for this, it's so resinous. Apart from mosquitoes there's not much on this planet as useless.

I can hear the river. There are boulders down there, left by the flood, which have landed all heaped together, making a crude dam. If the water's warm in summer you can have a jacuzzi downstream of them. Not today, though. Today is for huddling in warm clothes, sheltered from the mist that can still soak you through. There'll be months of this to come, months of short, damp days waiting for next summer. Next summer could be years away. Some years the seasons are two: a cold wet season followed by a slightly warmer wet season. Then cold and wet again. The mushrooms don't seem to care. This year they're more abundant than usual. I have them at home, packed in oil, pickled in brine, dried, cooked and frozen. I've got a year's stash. I'll have them in spring and early summer when no one else has them. No one ever thinks ahead here, plans for the winter or the spring lack of mushrooms. They don't bottle, preserve, make clamps for root vegetables. I read once that if you don't plan ahead for the winter in Finland, you won't be there in the spring – not alive anyway. Only the planners are left at the start of each year. The feckless, the lazy and the hopeless drunks have selected themselves out. Here I'm a one-eyed king in the land of the blind. I pick my mushrooms on the public highways, in picnic spots, on footpaths. Sometimes I find mushrooms that have been kicked over. I don't care if no one else bothers with them, it means more for me with less effort. I don't have to share my mushrooms with anyone else.

The river bank is wide here, twenty yards of grass before the forest starts. Riders cross here on their horses, I can see the hoof prints they've left as they've scrambled up and down the banks. I ride here when I'm not mushrooming. I can ride for twenty miles without using a public road, take the forest track from my home and complete a huge circle over hills, streams and valleys. I like to ride alone with my thoughts. In the summer flies surround me and I wonder; you canter a bit and the flies are gone – stop and they're back around your head again. Are they the same flies?

Travelling like this, in spurts and stops, is when I look for answers. Is it the travelling or the getting there that matters? I decide I like the here, even though it takes me longer to get there, wherever that may be. I know people who rush through the woods looking for mushrooms, in a hurry, seeing nothing. The trick is not to cover acres of ground, but to look about you where you stand. Really look. Then you'll find. Like I say, they hide from people.

I sit on the banks and watch the river flow. I think of Carlos Castaneda and Don Juan. Don Juan made Carlos stare at the water until he saw the spirit of it. I stare at my river, the river that visits me, willing its spirit to make itself known to me. Maybe it only works if you've eaten jimson weed. I don't think datura grows here, and even if it did, I'm not sure I like the sound of what it did to Carlos. It's mesmerizing watching the swirls and eddies, the sound of the cascade is deafening if you let it be. Which is the river? That bit coming or that bit just gone? I decide to work it out. I throw in sticks and time them over twenty paces. My river is flowing at nearly five miles an hour. Say five. It's about twenty-five miles to the sea. In five hours this bit of river will be sea. A whole new bit will be here, and it will still be my river. I remember Eliot: 'I do not know much about gods: but I think that the river is a strong, brown god.'

I've been out for three hours now, and I still have no ceps. I'm regretting leaving the honey fungus behind. What I have in the basket is OK, but it's not premier-league. I want ceps. I wade the river downstream of the boulders onto a stony beach which slopes gently up to the other banks. This beach is also a remnant of the great flood. It's all changed – there were the remains of an old stone bridge here going who knows where. It's all gone now, there's only the pebble beach. I knew this when it was antediluvian; I often wondered about the bridge. There must have been a track to it once, but there's no sign of one. Just the piers of a stone bridge. Now even they're gone, not a trace left behind, only memories.

A fish jumps, a trout. There are lots of trout in my river, tiny brownies that never get big in the acid water. I don't really hunt fish, I don't have the touch with fly and line, I don't understand the trout; I don't love them enough to want to catch and eat them. Sometimes they would come down my mill-race to my water wheel and get stunned while turning in the undershot wheel. The dog used to eat them. Once this river had plenty of water wheels along its length, grinding grain, doing work, making money for their owners or creators. All were undershot wheels, except for one whose remains are still there. It was a horizontal wheel, whose drive shaft came up out of the water. Maybe it worked well. Mine is a breast wheel, part overshot part undershot. I made it because I was told it couldn't be done, that it was not economically feasible to build a small wheel with a small output. All the books said so. I built one, it turns with a pleasing slap-slap-slap that I can hear from the house. It lights one bulb. I have an idea to improve it. I'll work on it when I get home.

I walk the bank toward the new bridge, staying on the paths, eyes down, looking for my brown-topped prey. Is that …? A leaf, a Coke can, an empty biscuit packet. People walk here, littering, kicking over mushrooms. Not today though, it's a weekday. They don't come out of the city mid-week; the few that do seem nicer somehow. No one on the path, no canoeists in the river, no ramblers. I did a stretch of the river in a canoe once, with a good friend from my teens who killed himself in his thirties. We did it in the summer when the river was a tame little stream, shallow and reasonable. The real canoeists come in winter after hard rain and run the white-water. They enjoy the danger and the speed. Not me. I don't take risks, I don't gamble. I like to plot my course and then stick to it. No surprises.

The path is worn to bare earth from thousands of feet tramping through in the summer. This part of the forest has easy access from the road. Tree roots are higher in places than the path now, and are rubbed smooth by passing feet. There is a lot of pine here, the odd oak marks the outside boundary of the new plantings. Mostly the path is of least resistance, taking a route that misses overhanging branches and boggy bits. Sometimes there are choices where the trees are spaced far apart. I knew I would, I had to. Perseverance always pays off. There, in the last place I look, are three good specimens of *boletus edulis*, the cep. I dust them down, pull off the leaf litter and put them carefully in my basket. Carefully and lovingly. I ease them gently from the ground, I don't bruise them or the mycelium roots, and then I just stare at them. They're beautiful, firm, scented and delicious. A prize worth waiting for. And there's another thing. Found them in the last place I looked. Of course I did, once I'd found them I looked no more.

I can go home now. I've got what I came for, so there is no need to be out in the cold and damp any more. It's a successful hunt, my walk is over. I don't go crashing through the forest undergrowth for fun, you know. It's tiring and boring. It's the hunt that makes me do it, like it's the hunt for pheasants that makes me fight my way through thick rhododendrons after the dog. When I think of some of the crap I've walked through just for the hunt, I wonder. Waist-high heather — that's the worst. Each step means bringing your foot up level with your belly-button before crashing it down again. Five hundred yards of that would crucify you. And for what? For a look at black grouse who heard your galumphing footsteps half a mile away? Maybe the discomfort is related to the value of the prey, but no grouse is worth that kind of pain.

I've often thought that prey in plenty means no one appreciates it. If mackerel were rare they'd be prized alongside swordfish. When I was a kid, before batteries were common, chicken was a treat. Now it's a staple. In the city guild archives there's a document saying that apprentices can be fed salmon no more than three times a week. Salmon must have been as common as mackerel then.

I take the path home with my haul. From the garden gate I watch thrushes pulling lumps out of my thatched roof looking for food. Like hens on a dung heap they scratch and eat, scratch and eat. More leaks for me. I'll have to deal with that soon.

© mushroom.man. May 1996.

This was the first piece that I'd found by the mushroom.man. I'd been exploring the i-way and I'd found it by accident at http://www.eol.com/alt.stories/mushroom.tale. There was no address, it was just a piece of prose posted onto an electronic bulletin board; a bit-stream, waiting there for anyone to read.

I had recently discovered a passion for mushrooms, more by accident than by design. During long, lonely walks through the woods and fields I'd begun picking up the odd specimen and identifying it later from a book. After a while I'd begun to recognize the commoner edible species and even learnt how to cook them reasonably well. At first I thought of the net simply as a research tool, and I used it to find out all I could about mycology. There's a lot of people out there passionate about mushrooms, a vast selection of books and literature both scientific and mythological, as well as some very bizarre theories. The mushroom piece caught my interest. Whoever had written it knew about mushrooms. I found myself as interested in the author as in the piece, so I decided to make contact. I left a message on the bulletin board titled 'mushroom.seeker' leaving a brief hello and my address, gbarmstrong-@iow.uni.

Three days later I got a reply — polite and brief. Thanks for the message and the compliments. It finished with NRN, no reply necessary, and I wondered if it had a subtext of 'don't bother me again'. I was new to the Internet, and was still learning its manners and customs.

Having made contact I became even more curious. I read the piece that I'd found again, looking for clues about the writer. On the net gender is often the first disguise, but I felt sure this was a man. I tried to guess where the mushroom.man lived — what state, what country. Was this some old drug-crazed hippie? Sounded like it. Male, definitely. I put my reservations aside and decided to post another message.

Amanita muscaria. The Fly Agaric.
Large, conspicuous mushroom. Cap to 8 inches diameter.
Bright red cap with white warts.
Especially under birch and beech. Early to late autumn.
Strong hallucinogen. Used as such throughout history by many cultures.

two

Attn. mushroom.man.
Subject: NRN.
20 May.

Mushroom.seeker thanks mushroom.man for the e-mail. I know what
NRN means, but curiosity has the better of me. I feel that I'm only
beginning to discover the joy of mushrooms. They are obviously some-
thing you care about. Please tell me more, even if it's only something
about yourself.

It was brief, I thought, and to the point. I knew that many net users
were unhappy about having their mailboxes filled with unsolicited mail,
but my message seemed polite enough, and, after all, it could always be
ignored. After I'd sent it I checked my mailbox every day, sometimes
more than once. I was reminded of a time when I was twelve and I had
a pen-pal in Chile. We wrote interminable letters to one another, confid-
ing our innermost thoughts, writing things about friends and parents
that would otherwise have remained unvoiced. Like any essentially arti-
ficial arrangement it just sort of petered out.

Maybe the net is the same. People stumble upon one another elec-
tronically, your persona can be what you will. You become only what you
say you are; there are no other cues available for another's assessment.
Names, too, become a shelter. Like mushroom.man or mushroom.seeker
– you are only that part of you that you choose to divulge. A stream of
bits connects you to other bit-streams, a two-way electronic dance in a
reality beyond the daily. It's almost like choosing a character in an

adventure game; you move your character around an artificial world,
exploring, looking, interacting with what you find.

In the vastness and the anonymity of the net I suppose I hoped that
I'd found a friend — or if not a friend, at least someone with whom I
could correspond on a subject that we both found stimulating. I felt a lit-
tle foolish, checking my mailbox so frequently; like a child waiting for a
special offer. Still, my urge to make at least one friend overcame my
reserve. I didn't have to wait long.

A week later I got a reply. This time there was a slightly longer mes-
sage from the mushroom.man explaining that if he was going to send
me anything in the future it would be sporadic: he had no desire to
make a commitment. He'd appended a piece which, he said, would tell
me a little more about himself.

Before I moved to the river and this house, someone took the
corrugated iron off the roof and put on thatch instead.
Probably someone from the city who thought that it looked
rustic. Stupid bastards. Tin roofs don't leak, thatch does. It's
home to more rodents than the rubbish pit at the end of the
kitchen garden. The warmth I suppose. You can hear them at
night rustling around in the attic and in the straw. Sometimes
they're so noisy you'd think they were moving wardrobes
about. Some nights I sit with my rifle and shoot into the roof
at them. They go quiet for a bit, then the noise begins again.
I tried poison. They die all right, but you never know where.
The smell of putrefaction makes you look everywhere;
behind things, on top of things, underneath things. And
when you do find the rotting carcass you have to move it and
it always smells worse when you disturb it. I'm used to it
now. At least if you shoot one you know where it's died.

I found a rat in a kitchen cupboard once, trying to eat my
sugar. I fetched an old fencing foil with a pointed tip. I cor-
nered the rat and it faced me hissing. I skewered it with the
foil. As I pulled the foil out of the cupboard I lifted the point.
The rat slid slowly down the blade toward my hand squealing like a stuck pig, wriggling, squirming and bleeding.
There's no easy way to kill them.

Thatch is a philanthropist's roof. It gives pleasure to the passers-by, not the inhabitants. Tourists stop here in the summer and photograph it, bus-loads of them. It's no surprise that at the turn of the last century when slates got cheaper people pulled off the thatch and put on slates, because slates work. Mind you, a new thatch works as well, but it's not new after a year. It starts to leak again; first around the chimney, then along the ridge, then runs begin to form there, then the thrushes come and then it leaks all over. Thatchers aren't easy to get and they're not cheap. You have to patch and thatch yourself. The straw's a problem. Nowadays there is no long straw. It's sprayed to stunt its growth so it'll be easier to combine and less likely to flatten in winds and rain. It's the only straw you can get and it doesn't last pissing time on a roof. It's a continuous job – I leave the ladder propped against the gable, ready. Go up the ladder and look along the eaves, you can see the rat holes. The grease from their fur builds up on the straw at the openings. You can see it. They should never have taken the corrugated iron off. And there's rat shit in the straw. I've heard of people who've died of Weill's disease – you get it from rat's piss. You can't see it in the straw but it must be there. Where there's shit there's piss. One of these days I'm going to put the corrugated roof back on.

I'll tell you something else you get in rotting straw: mushrooms. They grow on the roof as well. They turn half-rotted straw into compost – the mycelium runs in thick, white clumps through the wet thatch. Insuring a thatched house is expensive; they say it's a fire risk. I defy anyone armed with a gallon of petrol to set fire to mine. You might as well try to burn a sodden bog.

As well as mushrooms in the roof I've got them in the house. They grow out of the skirting board in the bathroom. Huge pink ears of fungal growth. Occasionally I cut them off with a sharp knife, but they keep coming back.

There was a spectacular one in the kitchen. It's gone now, died when I fixed a leak above the kitchen ceiling. All that's left is a dark stain where it was. It's moist and humid in the house – it's old and has no damp course. What doesn't come in from the roof comes up from the ground. When I walk in I can smell the fungal spores. They're in the air, on the walls, in the cupboards. I can smell them on the clothes in my bedroom wardrobe.

It's a dark house with small windows. Even in the brighter days of summer the sun hardly ever gets in. I keep the range burning all year round. A moist, humid house. Good for fungi of all sorts. Even yeasts. Bread goes mouldy fast, green spots grow through a loaf in days. Sometimes I eat it anyway, it can't be any worse for you than penicillin. I'm aware of the fungi in the house, outside the house, in the air I breathe. Spores surrounding me like a bath, on my skin, in my lungs.

You can't get away from shit outside the city. It's in the fields lying in pats; rabbits shit everywhere, so do deer. I can even see fly shit on the bare light-bulb in the kitchen. The dog uses the garden as a lavatory, uses it broadly, never in the same place twice. The cats do it everywhere. In short, it's hard to avoid. You have to adapt, lose your city sensibilities, realize that it's part of the environment. When I first came here I'd never seen a septic tank. Didn't know what it was, didn't know how it worked. I do now. I've rodded it, emptied it, replaced broken pipes leading to it: I've got to know shit well over the years.

It was hard at first. I wasn't equipped physically or mentally for life outside the city. I missed the night-life the most. At eleven o'clock at night I would get itchy, a gnawing sensation of boredom combined with the pent-up frustration of having nowhere to go. I was living with Jane then. She moved down with me, both of us looking for the good life beyond the city limits. At first she settled better than me, looking after the garden, planting herbs, picking wild flowers, bottling fruit. I was the edgy one, fidgeting and fretting, uncomfortable with myself. Back then I didn't know why; I just felt cramped and stifled. After a couple of years I began to feel more comfortable with myself, while Jane became less and less content. Everything began to annoy her; the rain, the mud, the rats, the leaks. The end came the day of a particularly heavy downpour. The rain came through the roof into the hot-press, soaking all the dry, ironed clothes with smelly, thatch-brown water. Jane freaked. Her white party frock that she had kept as a talisman from our old life was ruined. I remember she held the wet frock and cried, clutching it in her hands and rocking gently, silently, on a kitchen chair. I noticed her fingers had become thin and bony, like an old woman's. It was still raining heavily, the kitchen window was steamed up, all I could hear were the steady drips of the rain falling into a pot in the corner. She looked at me steadily through her tear-filled brown eyes: it wasn't hate that I saw, I saw a woman who felt let down. In her eyes I had failed her.

That night, after the rain had stopped, I made supper for us. I opened a bottle of wine, put on some music. I tried. Jane was silent, uncommunicative. Suddenly she spoke.

'I'm leaving tomorrow.'

'Leaving for where?'

'Leaving for good.'

I said nothing. Couldn't think of anything intelligent. We ate in silence. I couldn't stop looking at her; her face, her hair, a mole on her neck. I could smell her. I kept thinking that if she was serious, then these were sensations I was experiencing for the last time. I couldn't come to terms with her not being there, I didn't want to believe it, half convinced that even if she did go, she'd come back. She went to bed before me; I busied myself clearing up – giving her time to get undressed alone. It was dark in the room when I got into bed; she lay with her back to me and I put an arm around her, squeezed her breasts, lay against her back smelling her hair, made love to her. The last thing she said before she went to sleep was 'I'm still leaving.' I lay in the dark trying to make sense of it. Maybe I thought that making love to her would somehow set back the clock, make her change her mind.

I've thought about that night many times since. I wondered how she could have shared my bed, even shared an orgasm, knowing she was going. A last fuck. Looking back, she was probably right. Why not? What difference was one more fuck going to make to our lives one way or the other? The next morning I woke up to an empty bed. Jane was in the kitchen, her bags beside her, a coffee on the table. She was combing her long, black hair slowly. She asked if I would drive her into the city. I refused. I said I wasn't going to help her to leave my life. She got up, picked up the two bags and said she was taking the bus. I watched her shut the door. I poured a cup of the coffee she had made and sat down. I looked about me at the damp, peeling walls and my eyes stung with tears. I wanted to run after her and shout, 'You're right. I'll change. Just come back to me.' But I didn't. I just sat there for hours. I tried to remember things that we'd shared, moments of closeness, the times when things seemed right, but I just couldn't seem to picture any of it. It was as though none of my memories were visual, just recollections of feelings and sensations. I tried to picture her face, her clothes, tried to recall the smell of her, but it wouldn't come. It occurred to me that perhaps I'd never really known her, never really understood her needs and wants, never really considered her feelings, never really paid her enough attention. I felt ashamed that my memories were so inadequate.

I didn't see her for years. I heard she'd got married and was living in London with three kids. Married to an advertising executive. You can't get further away from here than that. When I first heard the news I thought she was trying to tell me something and then I realized she wasn't thinking of me at all – she was just getting on with living her life.

Since Jane there's been no one steady in my life. Women have passed into it, through it, and then out of it. I never really went looking; most of them found me – some moved their goods and chattels into the cottage. I like the way women make nests, keep things together, clean, bring in flowers. All things that I like, but low on my own list of priorities. I like the way women smell, I like the sound of their voices, their feel. I enjoy their company.

The only pub in the area is a weekend haunt for ramblers, bikers, hikers and families out for a Sunday drive. That's where I meet them. I have my place at the end of the counter, next to the snug. Sometimes I wonder what makes them talk to me. Maybe boredom. When I look in the mirror I find it hard to assess what my appearance says about me: other people's perceptions seem so arbitrary.

My problem is that the worlds I inhabit are becoming less separate, less discrete. The boundaries that keep them apart are dissolving; I seem to move almost at will between them, sometimes involuntarily. Sometimes I have no control. That in itself doesn't worry me. I like abandon: losing my consciousness in orgasm or drugs. But both of these have time limits built in to them. You lose control for a few blissful moments and then you get it back. You don't mind abandoning yourself for a moment, because you know, you believe, you'll get control back. Lose that certainty and you're looking at a journey with no signposts, no end in sight and no way back.

It's a question you have to ask yourself. Are you prepared to travel when there's a chance that you'll never return, never come home? It's a real possibility when you travel into the unknown. You can get lost there. If that's something that frightens you, then you should stay where you're comfortable.

I remember the day I met the mushroom god. It turned my life around – my priorities changed, my world view was shattered, my ideas of self lost all certainty. I used to come to these hills at the weekends and eat my mushrooms. At first I tried to find myself; that is, tried to find the point of awareness that I called 'me'. I soon learned it was a hopeless task. There is no vantage point, no place from which you can observe that cannot be observed itself. All that changes is the viewing point. I thought of these points as islands, floating in a limitless universe. I would sit on one and observe the others, then on another, where I would have not only a different perspective, but could also see where I had just been. Perhaps that's what mystics mean when they say all is flux. There really is no hard centre from which awareness emanates.

It took a long time to get to where I am now. The day-to-day world kept on impinging, forcing me to forage for food, meet people, make a living. Most of my time was taken up with the simple exigencies of life, no time to think, to explore. At night I was tired, the best I could do was get stoned and listen to music. The business of living left little room for anything else.

Even here I need money, but not as much, not as often. When I need money now I take people stalking or on walks in the hills. I show them the burrows and sets, point out the plants and the trees, give the names of the mountains and lakes. Some of the city people seem to have lost all their physical abilities. A fence is a major obstacle, a ditch an Olympic hurdle. They remind me of the battery hens that I buy when they're past their laying prime. They take forever to come to terms with their freedom, they still behave as though they're battery-bound. I was once given a peahen that had spent its life in a cage. I carried the cage to the back garden and took the bird out. For a week she walked around in a tiny square, four foot by two, the size of the cage. Couldn't deal with the fact that the cage had gone. You have to get used to freedom, make your accommodations with it. Getting your horizons suddenly enlarged can be scary. The universe is a bigger place than you imagine – than you can imagine. And that's a problem. The short glimpses that I've had of its size are terrifying.

I used to come here at weekends just to take mescaline, acid, peyote. Occasionally Jane would come with me, but she never took anything – she'd just watch over me. Maybe she thought I'd do something stupid like the psychotics in the anti-drug shorts they used to make – try to fly and kill myself. Sometimes I'd wonder why she left that world to me alone; why she didn't want to share it.

Little by little these trips brought me closer to the natural world. I grew attached to the area. I associated it with freedom, while my apartment became associated with drudgery. The apartment was where I worked, where I received bank statements, paid rates. The hills were for letting my consciousness soar. I'd watch the kites as they circled and try to project myself into them, try to see myself as a speck on a hill-slope from a thousand feet up. They were the moments of freedom that made me give it all up for a life in the forests and hills.

I lost Jane along the way. She just wanted other things out of life, she took another road. That was eight years ago and it seems less of a trauma now. Back then it was; it took me a long time to come to terms with her absence. Moving had been a joint decision in every sense of the word; I began to doubt if it made any sense to be here alone. Slowly I began to redefine what being alone meant. It's not company that I need or needed – I can find that in the pub – it's someone to share things with; experiences, hopes and dreams. You need someone to be close to, someone who won't judge, who'll accept, who'll share. I haven't found that kind of relationship since Jane. I've found intellectual stimulation, sexual excitement and comforting bodily warmth, but never together. But then, as things have gone, it's probably for the best. There is no tie that binds me to any particular world and without that freedom the journey ahead wouldn't be possible.

Attachments are strange, illogical things. Not just to people, but to places. Why should a view of a mountain or a river valley exert such a pull? It comes down to how we define ourselves and our relationship to the world in which we live. The more attachments that you have to people and places, the more you are part of this world and the harder it is to leave it. Freedom comes with letting go. That's the traveller's way, not the way of the earthbound peasant. The peasant's world is the earth, it's on his skin, on his hands – it's his daily universe. To be free to travel you must have no ties: otherwise you go only to visit and you return again to your starting place. You must loose your ties not just to people and places, but to the world itself. But to untie yourself you must first find the ties, and that's easier to say than do.

That's what I've been trying to do. Isolate a tie and then try to undo it. Singly, one at a time. That's what makes me so angry about my roof. Somebody created an unnecessary tie that I inherited, and which binds me to a pile of rotting straw. First get rid of the obviously unnecessary ties, then work on the others. I don't take that to mean people. I'm not a hermit; I have no desire to be physically isolated. I have no wish to deny my body and live only in the mind. All I want to do is to have nothing that I care about so much that I can't leave. I want to keep my body happy, I'm not keen on mortification of the flesh; I might be taking my body with me. I'm not completely certain how the doors between various realities open and close. I still don't know what you can take through them other than consciousness.

The trouble with all this is that there are no reference points, you can't check your progress with anyone else. There are no physical markers that two minds can agree on. I've read what Huxley and Castaneda have said about alternative realities and some of it fits with what I've found and some doesn't. Just like a fifteenth-century mariner you find that no two maps show the same features. That the major land masses exist is not in dispute, just their exact location and properties. Each psychic traveller remembers different bits, sees different things, and describes it uniquely. Like early explorers, travellers to these worlds are few and their tales contradictory. I find myself asking, Did they really go there? Why is their description so different from mine? Maybe these worlds change and bend under the view of each traveller, showing only what that particular mind can digest. But then wise men and philosophers rarely agree on the nature of the reality that we all experience every day. If you can't get agreement on what is common to all then it's not surprising that a few find their experiences incompatible from time to time.

It changes you, mind travel. After talking to someone for more than a couple of minutes I can tell if they have or haven't travelled. There's a look in the eye; a feel. Travellers can recognize each other even without saying too much, so much is unspoken. It's a secret society; it's feared by many and persecuted by the law. I don't consider myself a pariah; exploring the largely unknown is a warrior's task, it needs fortitude and determination. If I can bring back information from where I go, then more knowledge is the result. Someone should map the dreams.

Whoever the mushroom.man was, he was shy of society. This infant correspondence with me may well have been the first interaction with someone else he'd had for a long time. That might account for his trepidation in starting it. That and his fear of attachments. It felt strange; I had the sensation rightly or wrongly that I was learning something intimate about another person, yet I had no idea who that person was, didn't know his name or what he looked like – all the things you would normally take for granted when getting to know someone. I began to realize that the net was a world with new rules, a place where only a piece of you could venture, a place where interaction with others demanded different protocols. At the turn of the century people had to learn telephone manners, a new etiquette to deal with this new means of communication. Talking to someone who wasn't present was a new concept. Dealing with people electronically has its own novel possibilities. I was sure that netiquette would develop in the same way.

Looking back on it now I suppose I pressed myself on the mushroom.man because I wanted some kind of human contact, and even this remote, asynchronous communication was better than none. Like someone looking at a scene of gore, I found myself partly repelled by what I'd read and partly fascinated. But this was the joy of the net – I was able to communicate only the reactions that I wanted to and keep the rest to myself. It solved another problem for me: on the net my natural reserve and shyness with other people wasn't a consideration. The normal rules of intercourse didn't apply in this new world of electronic reality.

Armillaria mellea. Honey Fungus or Boot-lace Fungus.
Small to medium size. 2-4 inches high. Grows in clusters.
White to yellow. Strong mealy smell.
On rotting wood. Summer to late autumn. Common.
Edible when cooked: good when mixed with better mushrooms.

three

I spent my free time increasingly on the net, not researching and learning, but sending e-mail to the new contacts in my life. It was like joining a club — some of the older members were accommodating and encouraging, others aloof and remote, answering my queries with form replies. I was beginning to feel at home with netiquette. The net became like a window into another universe, where from the security of my armchair I could look and interact with its denizens. A friend told me that it was like having a ham radio: you end up talking to people for no other reason than that they have a radio.

The truth is that my own life was in something of a limbo. I had just moved to the University of Iowa, where I was doing post-graduate research in behavioural psychology. Iowa was a very different world from the rural England that I had grown up in; its manners and customs still held fascination and a little awe for me. I had no close friends, no one with whom I could share confidences. I was a stranger in a strange land.

What made the i-way so attractive was that here was a world of people you could contact without having to dress up, without any social embarrassment. Here my strange manners and accent caused no comment. I could find forums where researchers like myself shared data and opinions, and I could find a kind of social interaction. I suppose I was simply lonely.

Part of my days involved teaching first-year students and giving tutorials, the rest in working on my own thesis. I had planned to examine drug dependency, treatment and recidivism, ranging from the physically *addictive drugs like heroin to those whose long-term effects were less well understood, like ecstasy and the psychedelics.*

I kept up contact with the mushroom.man, doing with e-mail what I knew I often did in the real world: using flattery as a tool to elicit more information. I told him that he wrote beautifully, that his ideas were inspiring. I encouraged him to send me anything he had written. The thought began to form in my mind that the mushroom.man could make an excellent subject for study. It occurred to me that there was something a little ignoble about using him as a case-study, but there seemed little harm in it. I kept asking for some more personal history and eventually he agreed to send me something. After three days it arrived.

College is where I discovered dope and acid. There was plenty of time to experiment and like-minded people to experiment with. Greg Holder was my soul-mate. He was studying computer science with me and was a mathematical prodigy. He didn't fit the stereotype; he was tall and broad with looks that women seemed to like. He had long, thick blonde hair which he wore swept back, making his broad, high forehead his most obvious feature. He had an easy manner and a warm charm that made men enjoy his company as much as women did. A classic Nordic type with blue eyes, but with a sunniness of disposition more readily associated with the Mediterranean. He had a consistency of mood which made his company comforting. He was predictable without being boring. In fact, his emotional balance was part of his attraction. He made life look effortless, in his studies and in his play. He had the uncanny ability to remain friends with his parade of ex-girlfriends; something I envied in him more than anything else. They all appeared to give him an unconditional love, even after he'd left them for another. We spent most of our days together, talking, smoking dope. He had a mind like no other I had met, endlessly questing and endlessly questioning.

In our first year he wanted to build a water-powered computer as a project. The idea excited him. It would be huge, slow, cumbersome and messy; but it could be done. All the primary logic gates would be built out of easily available plastic plumbing fittings. Not, and, or, nand, nor; all these logic gates could be made to operate on water rather than electricity. The point? Only that it could be done. It would need hundreds of thousands of gates, millions of gallons of water, millions of one-way valves. It would be a giant engineering folly, a monument to his crazy ideas. His enthusiasm was infectious; after all these years I still have a hankering to build it as a tribute to him.

We were close, like brothers. When we weren't finding out all we could about sex, drugs and rock 'n' roll we were immersed in the electronic reality of computers, trying to make a chip think. Neither of us had much time for the others in our year. They were dull, with no ambitions or horizons beyond the course and the prospect of a job with IBM. They were well suited to the donkey-work of programming. Never innovative, never trying new ways of coding, they simply ingested the textbooks and regurgitated them in an unimaginative spew of numbers. They were people you could sink a beer with, but only Greg stimulated my mind.

Artificial intelligence was our Grail; write a piece of code that could modify and replicate itself, learn from its mistakes. The idea was as absorbing to me as any philosopher's stone. It represented a whole new evolution of machine, something more powerful, with more far-reaching ramifications, than the invention of the wheel. It would revolutionize our world, change our relationship to machines and the environment. We were standing at the gateway of a new and unexplored universe, virgin territory waiting for us to go in there and tame it. We were Viking warriors setting out to explore and conquer. Without this vision the drudgery of number-crunching would have smothered me. I could do it only because I believed that there was a use for this tool beyond the mundane, beyond the pedestrian accounting packages that filled so much of our time.

If it is our intelligence that lets us create and relate to our reality, then what would be the reality of a thinking machine? How would it perceive its world? Greg believed that that would be outside of our programming. Once self-awareness had been generated, then what the intelligence was aware of would be beyond our manipulation. It would be the recreation of Frankenstein's monster, another myth made real.

How can you define intelligence? We know it when we see it, but it's hard to pin it down to a definition. If we meet an intelligent response to an action then we assume intelligence is the agent. Greg wrote a simple program once that made conversation on screen with a human at a keyboard. He asked volunteers to assess whether they were interacting with a program or another unseen person connected to the screen by another computer. Most of them were sure that the seemingly intelligent responses were human. I suppose they were, in a way, since the program was the result of human intelligence. Yet an unthinking chip gave all the appearance of intelligence. Easy to confuse appearance with substance.

We tried to introduce these ideas into class, but the lecturers were prepared to tolerate only a brief discussion. They wouldn't let esoteric ideas interfere with the business of making machines fit for the business world. It was no accident that the world's largest manufacturer of computers called them Business Machines. Yet we knew there were places in the world where ideas like ours were taken seriously and funded well. Places where people talked of little else. Greg and I were developing our ideas in an intellectual vacuum. Occasionally there were snippets from the outside. I remember finding an article called 'The Chinese Room'. Suppose, it suggested, you have a closed room with only a door and a postbox. You post a Chinese ideogram through the door and an English translation comes back out. Is this intelligence at work? It looks like it. If I then tell you that inside the room there is a man with a look-up table, who takes the ideogram, finds its English equivalent and posts it back out, then you have to re-assess. He knows no Chinese at all, he does not even have to understand what he is doing, he is only following a simple rule. If we replace the man with a computer program then it is easy to see that it is the look-up table itself that is the product of intelligence. Observing the room from outside leads us to assume intelligent interaction, and yet it is entirely mechanical. Real artificial intelligence has to have more than the appearance of intelligence, it must be able not only to follow complex rules, but to generate new ones for itself. It has to be capable of interacting with its environment, even modifying it.

We spent hours arguing whether artificial intelligence could eventually lead to artificial consciousness. That was a step as large as the evolutionary one between a fish and a man. It also seemed to me to be a distinction that was often overlooked: intelligence and consciousness may be linked, but they're not the same. Greg believed that once an intelligent program could be devised, then it could modify itself generation after generation and might eventually become self-aware. I felt then, and still do, that without some kind of catalyst it couldn't happen.

I was sure that incorporating a database of known information into a program had to be the starting-point. After all, that is precisely how we school our young. Our work had to be making a system not only use the database according to intelligent rules laid down in the program, but to create a system capable of finding new relationships within the database not envisaged by the programmer. Simple beginnings, but these were the ideas that led us to where we are now. It was becoming clear to me that mathematics had a very real use beyond the theoretical. Using it to infuse thought into silicon seemed almost god-like. Take a planet and give it the code it needs to generate life from its own raw materials. I liked the analogy.

By today's standards the chips we had to play with were ludicrously small. I wrote a program once to play a simple game in 70 bytes; 72 bytes of memory was the limit for that little toy. In college we had mainframes, but we weren't allowed to play on them, and anyway, our time allocations weren't enough to allow for endless experimentation. We played with the first generation of programmable calculators, and then the first of the home computers. Back then 4 kilobytes of memory was considered massive. It was extraordinary how much could be made to fit if your coding was tight and compact. You couldn't be lazy then; if your code wasn't tight it simply wouldn't fit. You worked and reworked the code, tightening and shortening it until it fitted. But that was where you stopped. Once it fitted there was no need to tighten it further, so you didn't.

In the summer of that first year in college Greg showed me a package his cousin in California had sent him. Eight little buttons of peyote. He had a plan for them. He had organized a loan of a van from his brother who worked as a carpet-fitter. He thought we could go into the mountains and try them, away from the city, at the weekend. He was concerned that it might produce effects that we wouldn't be able to handle, so he wanted to bring his current girlfriend along to keep an eye on us. I didn't know her well, but I liked her. Her name was Jane.

Greg called around to my flat the following Saturday in a blue VW van. I got into the back and made myself comfortable on a roll of carpet. Greg handed me the buttons of peyote and I set to work removing the tiny, silken hairs from the underside of each of them. We had been told that the hairs contained strychnine, and were best not ingested. I finished plucking them off and asked Greg when we should eat the buttons. 'Now', he said, stopping at the side of the road, and we ate them, washing them down with orange juice while Jane looked on. Her hair was in plaits that she had wound into a bun at the back of her head. It showed off her long, slim neck. Briefly it occurred to me that she looked like Heidi. As Greg drove on I waited for effects, but nothing seemed to happen.

We arrived in a small village where Greg said 'I think this is it. There's a path down to the river somewhere near here.'

Jane suggested we ask in the shop outside which we had stopped. She got out to go in and Greg I followed. An elderly woman eyed us through thick glasses. Suddenly I saw the three of us in this village shop – Jane with long boots, a short miniskirt, a tiny tank-top with no bra; Greg with long blonde hair and a fur jacket; and me, hiding behind them.

'You here for the pageant?'

As Jane said no, a wave of explosive laughter came from my stomach. Greg's shoulders were shaking as he tried to stifle a laugh. It didn't occur to us to go outside and leave Jane to it, we just stood there, quietly convulsed, as the woman gave Jane directions while staring at us as you might at two escaped loonies. We came out of the shop and I was surprised to see that the van had a luminous halo around it. It was working.

I had had moments like the one in the shop when tripping with acid. More often than not these moments had reduced me to a sense of panic – inability to deal with money or answer seemingly bizarre questions. Things became impossibly complicated with acid. I remember walking home once in the early morning, tripping, when a policeman on a motorbike stopped me.

'Where are you going?'

'Home.'

He cocked his head and eyed me beadily, knowingly.

'Don't let me catch you walking this road again.'

He rode off, and left me in a state of complete panic. How could I never walk the street again? I couldn't stay in my flat forever, I'd have to go out from time to time, to college, to get food. How could he ban me from the streets? It was hours before I got over it.

This time there was no panic, just a sense of elation and control. It didn't matter how the shopkeeper perceived me, or anyone else. I felt god-like and peaceful. We found the river and walked in silence, slowly, savouring the smells, the sounds. The wooded banks were in full leaf, the river gently flowing. It was a perfect idyll and it infused me with a sense of belonging that I had never felt before. I stopped at the water's edge and scooped a handful of water into my mouth. It was cool and good. I looked around; Jane was standing there, looking at me, but Greg had disappeared. There was a fleeting moment when I panicked that I might panic, then a twig hit me on the head. I looked up; Greg was standing on a branch some twenty feet above me grinning, like an arboreal ape. I was puzzled as to how had he got there without me seeing him.

'How did you get up there so fast?'

'Fast? I've been up here for ages.'

I looked at Jane. She smiled so sweetly, so calmly, that I felt at ease again. Clearly Greg and I were both wrong. We obviously had no sense of time. I found that both exciting and interesting. I wanted to find out more about time accelerating or slowing down. We moved through the woods along the river-bank, walking downstream, Greg and Jane hand in hand. I became aware of a sort of force-field around me that insects seemed unwilling to penetrate. I wondered whether that was always there or whether it was the peyote. I waited for the wilder effects I had read about, audio and visual hallucinations, cross-sensory stimuli – but none materialized. It remained a cerebral experience rather than a sensory one.

I remember that really profound ideas about time filled my thoughts. Time, I realized, was something measured by motion. Whether it was the orbit of a planet or the swing of a pendulum, it was entirely determined by movement. Change the motion and you change time. But that's it. All I can remember of the rest of the ideas is that they struck me as amazingly deep and intuitive. They were gone from my memory by the evening. That's one of the problems with universal intuitions induced by psychedelics, they seem so meaningful at the time but even if you do remember them later they're either banal or senseless.

We came to a grassy clearing where Greg and Jane lay down in the sun. I lay beside them, Jane between Greg and me. I closed my eyes and watched an amazing display of lights and shapes. It was a while before it occurred to me that this is not the usual state of things. I became aware of the noise of a flock of a sheep somewhere across the river. The bleating was continuous, like a complaintful child. Every bleat hit a different note, and I began to laugh at the strange whinges and grumbles. I heard Greg laugh.

'They sound like people trying to imitate sheep.'

I thought that idea just wonderful. A field full of people pretending to be sheep. I sat up and rested on an elbow. Greg and Jane were lying on his fur jacket, both smiling with their eyes closed. Her black leather skirt had ridden up and with a shock I noticed the white triangle of her panties. I lay back again, felt the warmth of the sun on my body and let the light show begin again.

After a while Greg got up. 'Come on, let's go.' His decisiveness meant no dissent. We followed. We went back to the van and he set off, not saying where he was going, Jane and I not asking. He turned off the road by a gate to a field and announced we would have a picnic there. Food was something I hadn't been thinking of, but apparently Jane had. Greg produced some badly made sandwiches and a thermos of tea, and we ate. Well Jane did, with enthusiasm. I found each morsel an interesting experience and savoured each one. I was convinced that a bite of sandwich was nourishment enough. I lingered over the soapy taste of the processed cheese, explored the texture of the bread with my tongue as it slowly became a sodden lump in my mouth. The tastes were astounding; rich, strong and fulfilling. Jane and Greg had developed the same halo I had seen around the van. An aura of golden glow about two inches wide surrounded them. I smiled and idly scratched my neck.

'Don't do that,' said Greg, 'you're tearing your flesh.'

I stared at my fingernails, looking for blood or torn skin. Jane burst out laughing, a high, orange coloured, tinkling laugh like bells.

'What's funny?' I asked, rubbing my neck.

'You both are. Neither of you have a clue about what's going on.' She laughed again, warm and orange. 'Look, if neither of you two want this sandwich, I'll have it.'

'Have it. I've eaten loads.'

'So have I.'

I don't remember the afternoon well; only that we explored more woods and built a fire on the banks of what I thought was the same river. Greg was sure that he could call trout to him, make them come to shore to be picked up the way the Imragen call dolphins into shore to club them to death. It didn't work, but the fire was good. It was cool by late afternoon and Greg gave Jane his fur jacket. It was longer than her skirt, and from behind she looked as though it was all she was wearing.

Greg asked me to drive back to the city and he and Jane got into the back of the van. I took the coast road, as I wanted to watch evening fall over the bay. I parked in a car park on top of a hill used by young lovers with cars. I watched as the last speck of sun disappeared below the horizon and slowly began to illuminate the clouds from below with a soft orange light. Greg passed me a joint and I inhaled gratefully, enjoying the view and an inner warmth that had been with me all day, but that only now was I beginning to notice. Obviously we had not eaten enough peyote to get the full psychotropic effect, we'd been gently stoned but never out of it. But it had been a good day, with enough peyote to at least have an idea of what a larger dose could do. It was very different from acid; it had none of the sharp-edged feeling you get when you're tripping. With acid it's like there's a transparent crystal skin on reality that gives you the feeling of fragility. Rightly, I suppose. Reality is a fragile thing. I took another draw on the joint and turned in my seat to pass it back. Greg had made a bed out of the carpet remnants in the back and was lying beside Jane, kissing her, with his right hand between her legs. I turned back quickly and took another pull of the joint. Jesus. Right there behind me.

'Hey, don't bogart that joint, pass it back.'

I turned around again and saw Greg slowly remove his hand from between Jane's legs before he reached forward to take the joint.

'Are you lonely up there, by yourself?'

'No, I'm fine. Just looking at the view.'

'Why don't you come back here and join us?'

I turned around. Jane was smiling at me. Greg said 'Come on, it's too far to pass the jays.' I looked at Jane, and she nodded almost imperceptibly. I climbed through the front seats and found a perch on a wheel arch.

'Not a bad little bus, is it?' said Greg.

'Great.' I said. 'Good bus.'

He busied himself rolling another jay. Jane looked at me, then sat back, drawing up her knees and locking her arms around them. From where I sat her legs looked smooth and

41

long. I studied her face. She had brown eyes with long lashes, strong eyebrows, a neat nose and a small mouth with lips a little larger than normal. She had let her hair down, and it spread out behind her on the rolls of carpet. She caught me looking. I looked away.

Greg offered me the joint to light. I had nothing to light it with; Jane leaned forward and handed me a lighter, her fingers lingering fleetingly on my hand. I passed her the jay. She took a long drag and said, 'It's getting cold.' I started to move.

'Do you want to go?' I asked.

'No, I don't, it's nice here. But we could do with a blanket.'

Greg unrolled a rug and said 'This'll do.' He arranged another roll as a bolster pillow and he and Jane lay back.

'Come on, lie down over here next to us.'

'I'm not cold.'

'Come on. It's cosy here.'

I'm not now, nor was I then, particularly self-conscious. I was, however, very stoned and this was not an altogether straightforward situation. I suppose I assumed that this was normal for them, even though it was unusual for me. A little clumsily I lay down beside Jane. There's not much room to lie three abreast in a VW van, and we were close together. Greg rolled another joint. I showed him the one we were still smoking. He nodded and kept on rolling. 'Gotta get ahead of the posse,' he said.

The rug was heavy and warm. The occasional car headlights shone through the steamed-up back window. It had to be dark. Greg pushed his way between the front seats and put on the radio. He climbed back and we listened to Radio Luxembourg. He lit the joint he had just rolled, and we had two going between us. Jane closed her eyes. There was a little light coming into the van from a streetlight, casting its orange glow like a sunset. He leant on his left elbow and looked down at Jane. Gently he put the joint to her lips. She smiled and inhaled, her eyes still shut.

'She's got lovely titties. Haven't you, my little chick?'

'Greg!'

'She has, you know.'

Slowly he pulled her tank-top up, looking at me. I looked at Jane who said nothing, kept her eyes closed and kept smiling. I watched as Greg very slowly uncovered one breast, then the other. Her nipples cast long shadows. Greg was right; they were beautiful. He began to play with her right breast, squeezing, rolling the nipple gently with his fingers. He bent down and kissed the nipple, nuzzled it, sucked it. With a jolt I felt Jane reach for my hand. She found my left one and placed it on her left breast. My head was swimming. I felt her firm nipple, kissed it, sucked it. Suddenly Jane was convulsed with laughter.

'Must be what it feels like to breast-feed twins.'

It was a wonderful moment. We were no longer furtive, no longer unsure. This felt good, and there was no reason to be ashamed. It was fun, pure joy, giving and getting pleasure with no rules. Greg sat up, stripped off his shirt and slid off his jeans and underpants. His cock popped out as he slid them off, and he laughed. 'Ready for action.' I lost no time in stripping off and got back under the rug. Jane slipped off her skirt and panties without getting up. She kept her eyes closed as Greg eased her tank-top over her head and threw it at the roof of the van with a whoop. He was kissing her, while moving himself on top of her. Soon the van was rocking and creaking while I watched them fuck, right there in front of me. Jane's hand reached out and stroked my chest. Gradually her hand moved to my stomach, stroking my skin, her nails scratching lightly. I couldn't wait; I took her hand and put it on my cock. She didn't object, she began squeezing and pulling it in time with Greg's pounding. He came noisily.

'God, that was good. Really good.' He rolled off her and lay back. 'Fucking brilliant.'

Jane rolled toward me, giving me a nipple to suck on. I tried to put my hand between her legs, but she pulled away. 'No, not that,' she said quietly, 'just relax.' I could see Greg looking over her shoulder as she gave me a hand-job. When I came I watched in amazement as it squirted at least a foot into the air – the most explosive orgasm I'd ever had.

We just lay there after that, unselfconsciously, enjoying the flush. It was hot in the van now and the rug was thrown off. I could see all of Jane's body; her smooth belly, her long thighs with skin as soft as satin. It was good, just lying there, still feeling her breasts from time to time as though to make sure the right to do so was still mine.

We didn't go home that night. Didn't want the spell to be broken. Before we went to sleep Jane reached out and took a cock in each hand.

'Look, Mum, one in each hand!'

That's how we fell asleep. Me and my friend Greg, joined together by the arms of a woman.

This wasn't what I'd expected from the mushroom.man, but it was at least personal. Also it confirmed, assuming this was biographically accurate, that the writer was a long-term user of psychotropic drugs, which made what he had to say of interest to my research. At least, that's how I reasoned it to myself. But there was something more to it than that. This correspondence was opening up vistas into worlds that I knew little of, worlds of which I had had no previous experience. Each time the mushroom.man sent me one of his longer pieces of prose I felt like a peeping Tom; I felt a vicarious frisson as I read them. All my life I had been brought up to believe in Methodist virtues, in cleanliness and godliness. In some ways when I read his writings I felt as I'd done the first time I'd been lent a well-fingered copy of Playboy *at school. It wasn't just the three-colour exposed flesh that was so titillating, it was the added bonus of secretly breaking taboos.*

I was also aware that perhaps I was discovering in myself a nostalgie de la boue — *that strange yearning for the smutty, the dirty and the profane. I kept my printouts in a locked drawer, they were my secret, my clandestine stimulant. Perhaps I thought that the distance, the remoteness from the morally reprehensible, would make me safe from contamination. I could savour it, but be sufficiently removed that it wouldn't touch me. Like a man who thinks he can research the vice trade and keep his virginity.*

Lepiota procera. The Parasol.
Large mushroom. Cap to 10 inches.
Whitish with darker shaggy scales.
In pastures. Summer to autumn. Common.
Edible and good.

four

Increasingly I wondered where the mushroom.man lived. Outside of a city, clearly, but where? I wasn't even sure if he lived in the same country as me. A web site is a web site; it can have no geographical pointers. It can be anywhere.

I was aware that my behaviour was becoming obsessive. I felt like a pest, I kept e-mailing him, asking questions, looking for more to read, trying to find out more about him. He became quicker with replies, but there was always a sense of holding back. The long pieces that he'd sent me were somehow at odds with the shorter messages. I just felt that the pieces were honest and open, but that the messages that accompanied them were reserved – almost guarded. It was a curious combination, as though he could only open out in his impersonal prose.

There was an apparent chronology in what I'd got so far, as if he was telling his life's story. I clipped them together and reread them again, trying to get a feel for who had written it. It did occur to me that this could well have been a pointless exercise. Just because it read like an autobiography didn't mean that it was. It could have been pure fiction from start to finish, but deep down I didn't really believe that that was the case.

Besides, I was fascinated by communicating with someone who had no qualms about experimenting chemically on his own brain. Certainly I had never even considered that as a possibility; it scared me. My interest was purely intellectual – I had seen too many junkies in rehab.

Over the months I collected everything he'd sent me. But still the messages that accompanied his writings were impersonal, almost stand-offish.

Never the less I was enjoying the exchanges – I felt that somehow he was beginning to trust me with his very personal feelings. It was a strange sensation, meeting someone yet not meeting them. Establishing trust with nothing more than a name on a network. No background, no body language; nothing to go on other than the written word. I never showed the mushroom.man's writings to anyone then, I wanted to think of them as my research. But I started thinking about putting it together around that time, putting a bit of shape onto it all. I only wanted to maybe introduce it, and then let him tell his own story. Maybe I was naive, maybe this was post-hoc rationalization, but it gave me a reason for continuing the correspondence while keeping my precious sense of propriety intact.

I sat down on a warm June day and sent the mushroom.man yet another e-mail.

Attn. mushroom.man.
Subject: psychedelics.
8 June.

Your last piece of 28th May made interesting reading. You touched on the psychedelic experience but only tangentially. As you know psychotropic fungi are not my main area of interest, but I'm curious. Can you tell me more about the experience?

Two days later I had a brief reply.

Attn. mushroom.seeker.
Subject: FAQ.
10 June.

The questions that you ask can't be addressed directly. It's not that I can't explain, I can. The problem is that you won't understand. You ask me to explain in words what is essentially a non-verbal experience – it can't be done. You need some basic vocabulary first or nothing makes any sense. You can read about it, but it's no substitute for experience. Talking about transcendence is a bit like dancing about architecture. That said, this might answer some of your questions:

The hills attract a varied selection of people. Apart from those whose families have lived here for generations there are people who have drifted here for a variety of reasons; looking for peace, for fulfilment, for less scrutiny from the law. There are some whose personal histories are so odd, so startling, that they have all the marks of fiction and none of reality. It's not that I have much interest in their lives, it's just that I live here. I meet them, I hear about them in village gossip. Some even hit the national newspapers. There are no real threads binding them together; unlike those who live and grew up here, their only common tie is the place. There are no generation-long ligaments binding them to other families; they blow in, they blow out, like leaves in an autumn wind, rootless and transitory.

It takes time to put down roots, it's a slow process. Until you know your environment well you can't fit in, you can't put down roots. With no roots you just blow away. I think that holds true for other realities as well. It's very easy to get blown away. You need to find some kind of anchoring, a weight that stops the psychic winds from tossing you about. When Jane was here that was what she did for me. Kept my feet on the ground figuratively and literally. She was my take-off point and my landing pad. Perhaps it was a burden she never wanted. Come to think of it, I never asked her; I just took it for granted. When she left I had to do a serious reappraisal of my life. I'd lost my ballast; travelling was dangerous. It took a while to get used to it, not having her around. It was her company I missed, like the times that we sat in silence listening to the rain. Listening to it alone is simply depressing.

I missed the smell of her in the house, her things in the bathroom, her breathing at night, her warm body in the morning. No one major thing, just lots of little ones that add up to a life shared. Little habits, routines, small things too insignificant to describe; all these left with her. I couldn't take mushrooms, I just drank. Alcohol has no pretensions to enlightenment: drink enough and you get oblivion. When you feel like I felt, the road to oblivion looks a lot more attractive than the road to enlightenment. It's easier for a start, and there's no shortage of fellow-travellers in the pub willing to go down the road with you. You can drink yourself stupid in company. Those were the days when I began to meet the other hill-dwellers. When Jane was here we spent most nights at home, together. Didn't go out much, happy enough with our own company. At least, that's how it seemed at the time.

The pub here is all things to all men. Shelter for people like me, a stop for Sunday drivers, a meeting point for the displaced. I sat here for nearly a year, every night, my back to the snug propping up the bar. I could see all around with my back covered. It was my place, where you'd find me, my office. I watched the people come and go and slowly built up a picture of who they were and what they did. Until then I hadn't had much time for people. I just dealt with my life as well as I could and let them all get on with it. I felt like a biologist examining a new species. I was detached, an observer, trying to affect the patterns of transactions around me as little as I could to preserve their integrity, to stop me from contaminating them, changing them with my presence.

Things change when you observe them. I mean the act of observation is transactional. It makes a difference to what is observed. It's a problem. Nothing appears as it would if you weren't observing it. How you deal with that I don't know. Maybe when it's people you want to observe, you should use hidden cameras. If they don't know there's a camera they might behave as they would if unobserved. Like people in cars at traffic lights who think no one can see them. They pick their noses, finger out ear wax, do all those little things that are usually saved for privacy. I don't know if I learnt much about human nature, but I learnt plenty about who did what and when.

There's a lot of people here who for one reason or another found life in the city hard to take. There's a man who has an estate across the hill from me who ran a big financial scam in New York. He can't go back there, but he seems to have got most of his money out; he lives pretty well. Not far from me there's an old man who was one of the few Englishmen in the last war to defect to the Germans. He signed up with Wafen SS from a prisoner-of-war camp in Germany. I've seen his mail; he still gets the magazine for retired SS officers. Years ago, before I knew this, I met him walking in the woods. We started talking and the conversation got onto the war. He told me that the English had started civilian bombing and that the holocaust was a fiction. I was prepared to believe the first bit, but it seemed to me you had to refuse to look at a whole lot of evidence to believe the second part. This conversation made a lot more sense in retrospect when I knew his history. He was here, I suppose, because he had nowhere else to go.

I met Dutch Dave in the pub. He wasn't Dutch but he'd lived in Amsterdam for years. He was a Scot, but I never got to find out much about his history. Dave was small, thin and wiry. He had long thinning black hair which he wore in a pony-tail, and a droopy Fu-Manchu moustache. His movements were quick and twitchy, much like his mind. He was known locally as 'the weasel'. He'd rented a house not far from me and used to call by from time to time. He was a drug dealer; mostly hash and a bit a coke. I could only guess why he'd moved here. I liked him because he was inquisitive and bright, but he also interested me because he was so different from anyone else that I'd ever known. The world he lived in couldn't have been further from mine, and I suppose that was its attraction. I was fascinated.

I've never been very fond of coke and anyway I could never afford it. I always thought it brought out the worst in people – not individually, but socially. It was never upfront like passing a joint; always furtive, a nod and a wink, a trip to the lavatory. That was another thing, who wants a drug you take in a lavatory, using the cistern as a chopping board? I didn't like the effect on my jaw, the way it made me talk too much. Maybe it has its uses, but I could never see it as a recreational thing. Dave used it constantly and had a permanent sniff. I asked him why he did it.

'It's like driving a Roller, man. Makes you feel good, in charge, you can deal with things.' He took another snort. 'It puts your thoughts in order. You can concentrate better. You can drink more.'

I'd noticed that. Dave never got drunk. As soon as he felt the effects of the alcohol he balanced it up with a little coke. Then he'd drink more. Money was certainly not one of his problems. Maybe where to keep it was, and he had plenty to play with. I don't know why I liked his company; we had nothing in common, really. For me drugs were a tool to get me somewhere, for him simply a way of being where he was. I never saw him without his bag of coke, so I've no idea what sort of personality lived behind the white powder front. Somehow society seems to have divided its drugs: television for the poor, coke for the rich.

He came walking with me once when I was gathering psilocybins.

'You get off on these?'

'I use them.'

'You get high?'

'It changes my view.'

'Yeah. You get zonked, man. Bet you do. I could sell these. You find them, I'll sell them. Whatcha think? Eh? You'll make money – think about it, man.'

I did. I decided I didn't want to do it. Dave couldn't figure it at all. As far as he was concerned it was money lying there in the fields that you could harvest. He loved money, and couldn't understand why it held less attraction for me. In his terms it was a natural. You got it for free, and you could sell it.

'It's like a whore, man. You got it, you sell it – you still got it. These little babies just keep coming up out of the ground.

Money for jam.'

He never really let go of that one. He'd bring it up nearly every time we met. Eventually it got boring and I told him. He was huffy for a while, but another snort had him back to his bouncy self. I tried to explain why trading in mushrooms made no sense. It was like a religion to me. You don't trade in them.

'Tell that to the TV evangelists,' he sniffed.

It was Dave who introduced me to Hartfield Stanley. He was from Seattle, was very rich, and had recently settled in a mansion with a large estate attached, a little down the river from me. After he moved in, village gossip centred on where his money came from. There were as many versions as there were people living round about. No one really knew the truth and Hartfield was in no hurry to tell.

When he first arrived the centuries-old stability of our little community was stood on its head. He arrived full of New World fire. Within a month he had employed six new people from the village in addition to his cook and house-keeper: a driver, two gardeners, a shepherd to look after his pedigree sheep, and two farm labourers. The big house became the focus of much of our talk and a lot of our lives. He even persuaded me to work part-time, advising him on tree planting.

Whatever his view of life in the hills was, it was very dif-ferent from those around him. He embraced ideas and life-styles with single-minded enthusiasm and played them out to the extremes. Each new craze would last about a year and then it would be replaced with something new. When a craze was in full flow he would brook no interference, no distrac-tion. He had a whim of iron. None of these caprices took place in a vacuum; each one had to involve as many people as possible. Hartfield liked to share his crazes.

Dave persuaded me to come and meet him one afternoon when he was in the middle of his hunting phase. He greeted us in the hall, dressed as the squire: jodhpurs, boots, pink and stock. The large entrance hall had a log fire burning and Hartfield stood with his back to it, rocking on his heels and looking immensely pleased with himself.

'Join me in a stirrup cup,' he said walking across the hall. I looked at Dave.

'Stirrup cup?' I whispered.

'Shh.'

We followed him into what he called his morning room. It was a large room with huge floor-to-ceiling paned windows, bright and airy. Heavy mahogany and leather chairs were carefully placed near the bookshelves, each with a standard lamp nearby for reading. The room smelt strongly of new carpet. He handed me a glass of cherry brandy mixed with port. While he and Dave talked of the next week's meet I wandered over to the bookshelves, which were filled with half and full-bound books. Shelf after shelf of Norwegian titles. Hartfield saw me take one out, its pages still uncut after two hundred years.

'Aren't they beautiful? Some are over a hundred years old. Great workmanship. Look at that gold lettering. You really get the feel of a library from them, don't you?'

'They're beautiful,' I agreed, and put it back.

'Dave tells me you're into nature.'

'I suppose I am.'

'Take people for walks in the hills. Is that right?'

'Yeah. I do that too.'

'City people?'

'Mostly.'

He put his arm around my shoulders and led me back towards the drinks and Dave.

'We should go and look at my new horse. Wanna see her?'

We followed him back through the hall, through a rambling Victorian extension and out into the yard. On the far side I counted six stables, all with the half-doors open and all but one with a horse's head looking out. He took us over to a large bay with a white flash on her nose.

'This is Furze. She's my new girl.' He rubbed her under the chin. 'Isn't she beautiful?'

'A wee stoater,' said Dave.

'A what?'

'A stoater. A smasher.'

'More of your Scots vernacular, I suppose.'

'Aye, it is, so it is.'

Dave could switch in and out of his Scotsman guise with ease. Mostly he was indeterminate, but every now and then he became wee Davey fae Govan. Furze tried to bite Hartfield on the shoulder, so we moved away from the door. He looked at me, as though trying to gain some information from my clothes.

'Do you ride?'

'Not really.'

'Pity. You could ride out with us on Sunday. I've a spare horse now.'

'Thanks for the offer.'

'Come to dinner next week. Maybe I can persuade you to take up riding.'

'Thanks. Maybe you can.'

Hartfield decided it was time to get Furze tacked up and go for a hack. Dave and I left him, walking from the yard around to the front of the house. It was a large house, three stories over basement, the garden front covered in Virginia creeper. The gravelled drive, immaculately manicured, swept up to a Victorian *porte cochère* flanked on each side by four bays. An imposing façade, one that demanded a certain lifestyle.

'What do you think of him?' Dave asked as we came to the car.

'Seems friendly.'

'He's got more money than you've ever dreamt of. And he doesn't mind spending it. With a bit of luck I'll do a bit of business with him.' He rubbed his hands. It may have been the cold, but it looked vulgar.

'Is he serious about dinner? He hardly knows me.'

'That's the whole point. He's very keen to get to know everyone who lives around here. You included.'

'I'm not sure I'd have anything in common with him.'

'Think of it this way,' said Dave, 'you'll get a chance to see how the other half lives, and if nothing else you'll get a great meal for free.'

'Have you been for dinner before?'

'Loads of times. Well, two or three times anyway.'

I looked up at the brick and stone façade, my eye carried up to the huge chimneys topping the roof.

'Is it very formal?'

'God no. Bit of a piss-up really.'

I don't have a lot of clothes, and the ones I do are best adapted to the outdoor life. I wasn't even sure that I wanted to go to Hartfield's dinner party, but curiosity was winning. I am sufficiently self-conscious, however, to worry about what to wear. I didn't want to look completely out of place. I didn't mind looking a bit eccentric, but if I was going to go at all then I'd try to fit in, at least a little.

On the night, Dave called round to pick me up. He walked in as I was ironing a white shirt. He watched me intently.

'Domesticated little bugger, aren't you?'

'Have to be.'

'Hurry up.'

I had decided to wear the white shirt with my only tie, my brown cords and an old sports jacket. I thought that the combination would say rural if nothing else. We hurried out, and soon we were going up the long drive of Hartfield's house, gravel crunching under the tyres.

We were met at the door by Gordon, the butler, impeccably dressed in a black suit. He showed us through the hall, blazing with lights, into the drawing room. Through high double doors was an enormous room in which a small group of people lounged on sofas and on the floor. Only Hartfield was standing, his back to the fire. He was wearing jeans and a scruffy pullover. The effect of this alien environment was a little disconcerting, but I decided to make an effort. I'm glad that I did, because some of the people I was to meet there were later to haunt me. Hartfield strode over to us.

'Welcome. Glad you could come. Let me introduce you. This is White Cloud, my special friend.'

White Cloud lay across the front of the fire. I noticed that she was also wearing jeans, a tee-shirt with the legend 'Remember Sand Creek' and cowboy boots. She looked up languidly.

'Hi.'

'And this is Tony Modena, my agent.'

Tony sat forward and held out a hand.

'Glad to meet you.'

'And this is Betsy. Tony's wife.'

'Hello.'

'And Giles Montvert. Giles is French – from France.'

'Hello.'

'Françoise – she's here with Giles. And this is Elena.'

'Yelena, actually. Hartfield never gets it right.'

Yelena held my hand firmly and stared into my eyes. I stared at her odd turban. 'Don't be afraid. I know what you're thinking. I can read your thoughts, fears and desires. My grandmother was the famous Madame Blavatsky. I've inherited her gifts.'

I smiled and took my hand back in time to receive a glass of champagne from Hartfield. He moved back to the fire and held up his glass.

'A toast. To the new life in the hills. The Stanleys' new venture.'

I found a seat on a sofa next to Yelena. She was very keen on eye contact. I was still trying to take in the room and the relationships. Hartfield and White Cloud. Tony something and that woman with the tan. The Frenchman, Giles, and his wife. And Yelena. Dave was already in a tight huddle on another sofa with Tony. They looked similar – small, dark and thin. White Cloud was still prostrate, Giles had moved to the grand piano and began playing it quietly. Hartfield was still standing talking to the French girl.

'He's a composer.'

'Who? Giles?'

'Of course.' Yelena smiled. 'You can always tell when someone plays their own music. It has more soul than playing someone else's.'

'Ah.'

'Do you see the music? It comes across the room like clouds of colour. I can see it; look there – and taste it too. I have many gifts. You seem ill at ease.'

'No, I'm just getting a feel for the room. Trying to remember everyone's name.'

'Names are not important. It's who you really are that matters. I am Yelena, but I am also Catherine, a Tudor serving wench at the court of Henry VIII. I am also Indala, soothsayer to Cleopatra. I am many people, the sum of all their experiences. Yelena is just the label the world puts on us.'

'Ah.'

'Do you believe?'

'Believe what?'

'If you have to ask, then you are still unenlightened.'

'Can I get you another drink?'

'Thank you, no.'

'I'll just refresh mine. Excuse me.'

I stood up and Hartfield beckoned me.

'Let me top that up. Françoise and I were talking about horses.'

Françoise, that was it. Françoise the French girl. Like France. She looked French, very gamine, short cropped hair, thin – even her casual look was carefully contrived. Striking, but not pretty. I stood with them, sipping my champagne, listening to talk of hunters, rides and gallops. Yelena had moved to talk with the tanned woman, Tony's wife. Tony and Dave were still engrossed when Gordon came in.

'Dinner is served, Mr Stanley.'

No one appeared in a hurry to move – Giles was still playing and it seemed polite to listen. White Cloud got up and stretched. She was younger than Hartfield, I guessed around thirty, while he was probably in his fifties. She had a neat trim figure but surprisingly heavy facial features. A wide, broad face, large nose and a heavy jaw. Her eyes were dark and hooded, her long black hair was plaited in a single braid which hung down her back. She took Hartfield by the hand.

'Can we go in now? I'm hungry.'

'Of course, my dear. Giles is nearly finished.'

'Well I'm going on in now.' She turned to me. 'Are you coming?'

I followed her through the hall into the dining room. It was lit entirely by candles; in the chandeliers, in the sconces and on the table. I noticed that there seemed to be no electric light fittings in the room at all. It was candles or daylight in here.

'You're sitting here.' White Cloud showed me my place.

'How do you know Dave?'

'I don't really remember. He was just sort of there, if you know what I mean. He's been very good to me and Yelena.'

The others began to file in and I found myself once more next to Yelena. Opposite me sat White Cloud; Hartfield sat at the head of the table on my right. Dave and Tony walked in last, Tony rubbing his nose and sniffing. As we ate I became aware how attentive Hartfield was to White Cloud. He stroked her arm, held her hand when she wasn't using it to eat, filled her glass, made sure everything was passed to her. She seemed to take it as her birthright; never smiling, never responding. Her face remained impassive and not once did she address Hartfield. I was uncomfortable: Hartfield wanted to talk to White Cloud, not to me; she wanted to talk to no one as far as I could tell, and Yelena wanted to talk to me with lots of eye contact. Short of shouting down the table it was Yelena or silence.

'You are an otter.' She told me.

'Ah.'

'The otter is your familiar. You eat like an otter.'

'You mean fish?'

'No. The way you put food to your mouth. The way you look around quickly before you put a forkful into your mouth. Like an otter.'

'I see.'

'Why don't you look at me? Are you afraid?'

'No. I don't find it easy to look at you while I'm eating. It's not personal.'

'Look at me.' I did. I thought the turban absurd. Was it fashion or simply covering unwashed hair? 'You think me dangerous, don't you? I won't harm you, trust me. You live alone?'

'Yes.'

'I thought so. Like a badger in a set.'

'An otter you mean, surely?'

'Don't play with me. I am not to be trifled with. I am a Blavatsky.'

White Cloud looked at her intently, then said loudly, 'No she's not. She's Ellen Tranter. Not a Blavatsky anywhere in her family tree. I've known her since first grade; I should know.'

Yelena stared at White Cloud silently, as though making up her mind about something. She turned to me briefly.

'White Cloud? Bullshit. Mary Collins from Boston more like. What was it, Mary? Your great-grandmother was a Shawnee? Or was it great-great-grandmother? She's only been Rain Cloud since she met Hartfield.'

'White Cloud. And at least I've got native American blood. The nearest you ever got to Russia was a bottle of vodka.'

Hartfield looked edgy. 'Come on, girls. This is no place to

start an argument. We have guests.' He patted my arm. 'We all evolve personalities to suit our circumstances, don't you agree?'

'I suppose that's true.'

The two women avoided each other's gaze, both apparently struck by the pattern of the wallpaper. It may have been rude – bad manners perhaps to bring up the past – but it was hardly a major revelation. I thought no worse of Yelena. It really made little difference to me what their names were. I may not have changed my name, but I too was creating a new persona to live in. That's probably what stopped me from telling this absurd group of people how silly and shallow they seemed.

We spent the rest of the evening back in the drawing room where I became horribly drunk on seventy-year old Armagnac. I couldn't find any other way of dealing with the absurdity of the evening. I'd spent years trying to avoid banal conversations and empty-headed discourses and here I was surrounded by it. It may have looked glamorous to Dave, but it was simply unreal to me. It all seemed so pointless and contrived. Dave offered me a trip to the loo, but I was too drunk to want to move. I began to imagine that the room was full of cardboard cut-outs: Dutch Dave who wasn't Dutch, White Cloud who wasn't native American, Yelena Blavatsky who wasn't Russian – and what of me? Who was I? I was the mushroom.man.

Stropharia cubensis. The Starborne Mushroom.
Small to medium size. To 6 inches high.
White to pale yellow.
Habitat tropical in areas of high humidity.
Coprophagic, specially on animal excrement. Hallucinogenic.

five

The mushroom.man was right: I had no vocabulary to understand his thoughts on psychedelics. Well, that's not strictly true, I had an academic vocabulary and a huge library at my disposal, but I knew that wasn't what he meant. The only thing that really made sense was the idea of psychic weightlessness allowing the self to be blown around like a leaf in the wind. Since I'd come to the university that was a good description of what was happening to me. Without the contact and the support of my family and friends I felt rootless. I felt like a piece of flotsam, going wherever the tides of fortune took me.

The only goal I had formulated was using the mushroom.man as research for my own aggrandizement in the eyes of my peers. As much as anything this was my touchstone, and yet it too was being undermined by the mushroom.man. I felt that his last message was a little patronizing – explaining that he could tell me nothing because I wouldn't understand it. It annoyed me.

It occurred to me that the principal difference between me and the mushroom.man was a sense of place. He was clearly rooted to his geographical place physically and emotionally. I, on the other hand, was living with almost no sense of place or belonging. I was a traveller who had simply stopped for a while, but who would continue his travels soon enough. The feeling of 'just visiting' was probably what was keeping me from making real friends at the university while at the same time chasing an electronic friend across the net. Anyway, I continued the e-mails and he continued to reply.

Attn. mushroom.seeker.
Subject: personal history.
11 July.

I know little about you, other than your interest in mycology. But you are obviously computer-literate or you wouldn't be on the net. Given that, I thought this might be of interest:

Back in the city days I worked for an engineering company. It specialized in sensing equipment and was big and rich. They had decided to computerize the business, bought a mainframe and hired an operator. It was my first job and my introduction into what my supervisor called the real world. Tom Greenan, my supervisor, was a man in his early fifties who had worked all his life in the accounts department. He was short, overweight and balding. What little ginger hair he had was parted over his left ear and pulled across the top of his head like stray strands of coir embracing a boiled egg. He peered through thick glasses which made his eyes look tiny and piggy. He didn't wash much, his breath smelt of gum disease, and dandruff sat permanently on the collar of the crumpled blue suit that he never seemed to change. Apart from his physical unattractiveness he was stupid and aggressive. I now have a Leghorn cock that I call Tom because of his mindless aggression and inability to learn anything.

My job was to run the computer program that did the accounts. Dull donkey-work and badly paid, it would have been penance enough in itself without Tom breathing down my neck and in my face. The fact that he knew nothing about computers didn't deter him from constant interference. He was on my case from morning to night, kept calling me a witless hippy in what he thought was a jokey way, kept telling me to get my hair cut so that I wouldn't look like a girl. He should have been a prison guard. He couldn't really deal with the change. Because he had always filled out everything in triplicate he insisted that the computer print-outs did too. I couldn't make him see that it was pointless; the information was already saved in the computer's memory and could be retrieved at will. He just couldn't understand that the computer was a new way of doing his old job, not just his old job mechanized. No, it had to be done his way. Do you know what's it's like to work for an idiot? To have a complete moron have the power to organize your day, your life? It was soul-destroying, as relentlessly grinding as the task of that poor bastard Sisyphus.

One day Tom came to tell me that the company had decided to put its inventory on computer and tie it in with sales and ordering. I explained that our computer already had the capacity to do that. He told me that I was a witless hippy and that he was in charge, not me. I lost it; I told Tom all the things I'd wanted to, and went to see the boss. I explained to him slowly and carefully that I knew the machine well. That it was my job to work on it, that I knew how to set up the inventory – that if I could be left unhindered by Tom it could all be done in-house without the outlay of any more money. He seemed to take it in and told me he'd look into it.

What I didn't tell him or Tom was that the computer came already programmed with what they wanted. It was standard practice then, the entire accounting package was on the machine the day you bought it – nominal ledger, sales, ordering, final accounts. The computer salesmen didn't tell you that, though. You had to buy each module, and when you did an engineer would come and spend a day fiddling at the back of the machine, looking busy. All he would do was make a connection which I could have done myself. I knew this because the engineer that serviced it had been in college with me. He showed me how it worked. It was a low-level scam, and I thought that by explaining it to the boss I would earn some respect. Instead I was fired the next day. Greenan arranged for the company to spend a great deal of money and I was left with no job.

I didn't care, really. I got on the books of an agency and got temporary, short-term jobs. But the work was mindless and repetitive, there was no room for experiment or flair. Greg had gone to America. I got the occasional postcard from him with snippets of news. He ended up as a researcher at the California Institute of Applied Technology, doing what he always wanted, chasing the rainbow of artificial intelligence.

Jane and I were living together. We'd just drifted together after Greg had left for the States. It wasn't really a passionate affair, but it was comfortable. Despite what I'd imagined about Jane's sexuality, sex between us was never wild and uninhibited. It was, as I said, comfortable. We never talked about the night in the van, and even when Greg was still around it was never mentioned and never happened again. It was funny, after that night Greg and Jane drifted apart and she and I drifted together. Drift is an exact word, because it makes me think of tides moving things about, things that have no choice, things that simply go where they're moved to. It was a lazy way to start a relationship, and I suppose there was a fear that talking about the three of us could bring ideas to life that were best kept secluded. Yet that night in the van was important, because it first brought Jane and me together. Strange that we couldn't talk about it.

Jane had a job in a boutique that sold overpriced clothes to bored, rich women, and men who thought of themselves as executives. It described itself anywhere it could as exclusive, whatever that means. Anyone could walk in, so it wasn't exclusive in that sense. We lived without much money in a rented flat in what was once an elegant Georgian house. The area was run-down and full of cheap bedsits; no sense of community since people never stayed. Not any longer than they had to.

We used to talk at length about the hills. We saw them as freedom from the repetitive routine of daily life. We'd take the bus most weekends and go to the forests. I would take psilocybin and Jane would walk with me. She never took any; she said that she hated the idea of losing control. I didn't argue. Sometimes I thought it was wrong that she couldn't share it with me. I was increasingly comfortable in a world that she knew nothing about – that she wanted to know nothing about. It was an exciting world where I could let go, my mind racing around the universe gorging itself on all the new experiences that were there for the taking. Whenever I wanted to re-enter the world I'd left, Jane was there to bring me back. She got good at that, like one of those men with ping-pong bats that bring in taxiing aircraft. The week-ends in the hills were good; but the bulk of my days were not.

Looking back it wasn't dull. There were parties and visitors to the flat. Mostly we'd sit, get stoned and listen to music. It seemed like fun then, meeting new people, going to discos and generally cutting loose. But it nagged me that my work was nothing like I had expected. Maybe it's just that routine dulls the edge of excitement. I suppose that as usual it was Greg who became the catalyst for change.

It was early summer when Greg turned up unannounced at our door. He looked great; tanned, fit and rather prosper-ous. That sort of sleek look that comes with well-being. He'd been in the country for a week, but had been to see an old friend. He made himself at home at once and managed to create the illusion that it was like old times once again. He talked of sun, surf and Californian sex, his face glowing with health and fulfilment. He seemed to me to be a shade or two blonder. We looked weedy, pale and dull in our sorry flat and dingy clothes. Greg was burning with a passion for what he was doing and full of new and exciting ideas. That night over a couple of bottles of wine he talked of his work, dreams and mushrooms.

He told us about *psilocybe cubensis*, an American species of psilocybin mushroom that he called 'star-borne'. He had met the mushroom intelligence, talked to it about his work, learnt from it. It was a trade, he explained. The spores probably arrived on earth on a meteorite. They found the ecosphere to their liking and grew.

'You have to understand that the bit of the mushroom you pick – the bit above ground – is only the fruit. The beast itself is big, spread over acres, sometimes over square miles. It is a life-form like no other on this planet and is still little understood.'

When Greg talked to the mushroom the deal proposed was simple. The mushroom would give Greg and all mankind information about the boundless universe; in return it wanted no more than passage for its spores when our technology led us to interstellar travel.

Jane smiled indulgently, as though listening to the imaginative ramblings of a child.

'How do you talk to a mushroom?' she asked.

Greg took a breath, slowed down, realizing that he had run ahead of himself. 'You don't talk to a mushroom like I'm talking to you. It's not verbal communication. I say talk because that's the easiest way to describe it, but that's not what it is. When you eat the fruits – what I call the fruits of knowledge – you get a sense that somehow there is someone else present. Not another person, but another intelligence. It's not clear whether the intelligence is now part of your mind or external to it; it doesn't really matter. What's important is the sense of dialogue. That there is a real exchange of information between our way of thinking and an entirely alien life-form. It means, amongst other things, that we have to redefine what we mean by intelligence. If we define it in terms only of human understanding then only humans fit the definition. But that doesn't square with my experience of the star-borne mushroom. There is a very real sense of communion with another being. The fruit is only the gateway to meeting it.'

'You really believe that mushrooms come from space?' Jane asked incredulously.

'Originally, yes.'

'That's a little hard to believe.' She looked at me. 'What do you think?'

I looked at Greg's face, full of earnest evangelism. It was an interesting thought. I'd certainly never talked to a mushroom, and none had ever started a conversation with me. He seemed strangely vulnerable at that moment, desperately wanting approval and agreement.

'It's possible. I don't see that over billions of years there couldn't have been galactic coincidences like meteors bringing spores to this planet. Sure, I believe it's possible.'

'I think you've both done too many drugs. You're losing touch with reality. Sorry, Greg, I really can't believe that.'

'It's OK. You don't have to. Maybe I got a little carried away.'

'No, not at all,' I said. 'Tell me more.' I wanted to encourage him, give him support.

'Well, there's a lot more to this mushroom thing than most people will believe. There's this guy in Hawaii called Terence McKenna who's a genius. He grows psychedelic mushrooms, he knows everything about them, it's his life. You'd be interested in his ideas on the evolution of human self-consciousness, because it applies equally well to artificial intelligence.'

Jane got up and left the room. Greg watched her leave and turned back to me.

'You see, if you think of human intelligence as I do, as a kind of high-level program that gets passed on genetically, you run up against the problem of self-consciousness. How does the program become aware of itself? This is no new question, people have asked it for millennia. You can say it was God who did it, you can believe in visiting spacemen, you can believe it just magically evolved. Or you can believe Terence McKenna, like I do. Somewhere along the line some proto-hominids ate psychedelic mushrooms. That's not too hard to believe. Most simians eat mushrooms as part of their diet – the idea that they may have eaten psychotropic fungi is not far-fetched. If intelligence that is not self-conscious as we know it is like a simple reactive program – stimulus/response – then you have to have an external impetus to make the loop. Somehow the program has to loop back onto itself. It has to have a kick-start to do that, I can't believe it happens accidentally. Mushrooms make a simple explanation possible for an extraordinary event. How else can you explain that it needs such tiny amounts of psilocybin to completely change the nature of the brain's chemical bath? There's an affinity between our brain, its synapses and the mushroom that is physical as well as mental. It's already a part of our genetic heritage. That's why we respond so easily to it.'

Jane came back with three mugs of coffee. She handed one to Greg.

'Don't take it personally,' she said, 'I don't take any shit from him either.' She sat down and laughed. 'You can't expect me to take talking to mushrooms seriously.'

It was a long night. Greg had a lot that he wanted to tell us and there was a lot I wanted to hear. He had some grass that he rolled California-style, no tobacco and a single skin. 'Home grown,' he told us proudly. We smoked, we talked, we listened to James Taylor. I remember that night vividly, it was the night I decided to go travelling. Well maybe not right then, but the seeds were planted. We'd got comfortable, lounging on cushions, long pauses in the conversation. Tired, stoned and relaxed.

'Dreams,' said Greg, 'have you considered them? That's another reality that we all experience nightly. A whole realm of consciousness where the daily rules don't apply. If you could grasp hold of that reality as an actor, rather than as an observer, think what you could do. Anything would be possible, from the mundane to the bizarre. Travel to the places that you dream of, make love to your dream women, do whatever you want. There's a freedom there for the taking. There's a guy in California who teaches you to control your dreams; shows you how to inject self-awareness into them so that you gain control of where the dreams are leading. Think of that. If you can do it, then you're like a man staring at an ocean for years who is suddenly handed a boat. You can find out what's over the horizon for the first time in your life. Think of it, a dream traveller. An oneironaut. You see, it's all connected. The realities of dreams, drugs and daily life are part of a continuum. It's just that we can only see them one at a time. We see, experience, walls that divide them. Huxley talks of doors of perception. Our view is not uninterrupted; we have to find ways of opening the doors to these other realities. All this matters to me, because it's all information that I use when I think about artificial intelligence. If I don't have a clear idea of what perception, intelligence and awareness are all about then how the hell can I hope to create it?'

There was more of this monologue, but that's the gist of it. I was too stoned to make it into a conversation and I think Jane was too. All the while he talked I couldn't help reflecting on my life. I looked around at the dreary wallpaper, the dusty paper lampshade, the coffee stains on the carpet, the secondhand sofa and chairs. Briefly I toyed with the idea that even Jane was a cast-off, but dismissed it. It was a line of reasoning I didn't want to follow. And tomorrow? Tomorrow I would have to deal with yet another Tom Greenan; same ilk, same ignorance, same aggression. Stupid parties where you drank too much and got sick, nights spent with the same people none of whom had Greg's fire or breadth of vision. I watched him while he talked. We'd had the same start, he and I, and yet he was riding a wave, surfing joyously through his life. Why was mine so bloody humdrum?

He stayed on the sofa that night. Before we went to bed we decided that the next day would be a day in the hills even if it meant Jane and I would miss work. We got up late and ate a leisurely breakfast. Greg was quiet, but I put it down to a hangover; I wasn't feeling too great myself. The combination of the two – weed and alcohol – can be debilitating. Greg had hired a car, a further sign of his material success. I couldn't even afford to run a motor-bike. We hadn't gone far when he announced he had to pick something up. He called into a house, greeted the owner warmly, and emerged with a roof-rack and a canoe.

'Didn't I tell you?' he grinned as he got back into the car. 'We're going canoeing.'

The day was grey and damp, but we arrived in the hills to find that the rain had stopped. It was still threatening, but dry. We parked by the river and got the canoe to the shore. Greg went first, tossing me the car keys. 'Meet me at the next bridge.' Jane and I drove about two miles downstream to the bridge and waited. The river was low, no fast white water today. All the better, since I'd only ever been in a canoe on a lake. I stared at the river and decided that I could handle it.

'Good to see Greg again, isn't it?' said Jane.

'Great.'

'He seems to be very happy. I mean, he seems to have found something that suits him. He looks well.'

'Yeah. He does.'

I watched a pair of dippers going about their business in, on, and over the river bed. What was she thinking? Last night she had refused sex, saying she was too tired. She did-n't go to sleep, though. I knew she was awake, because I was. I could hear the way she breathed and it wasn't the breathing of sleep. Something was on her mind.

'Do you miss him?' I asked.

'Miss Greg?'

'Yes.'

There was a long pause. I watched the dippers. I began to think she wasn't going to answer.

'I suppose I do, yes.'

'So do I.'

We waited in silence. How long does two miles in a canoe take? It seemed forever. Eventually we saw him rounding the bend in the river about four hundred yards upstream. I went down to the river.

'God that was good. Your turn, old buddy.'

'What about Jane?'

We both looked up at the parapet.

'Not me. God no. I'd get soaked.'

'Right,' said Greg, 'you take it down to the next bridge, and we'll meet you there.'

The next bridge was about six miles downstream by road. God knows how far by river. I'd never been down it before. Most of the way the going was easy, slow lazy bits of river that needed no concentration. I was able to look at the banks, the forests, the occasional field of sheep. A heron took off lazily as I rounded a bend. Where the river got wide it became so shallow that there were times that I had to do a kind of bum-shuffle, pushing down on the river-bed to make the canoe slide onwards. One place was awkward. There was a pile of huge boulders blocking the river, mak-ing a dam that I was not prepared to shoot. I carried the canoe downstream and started again. I thought in the silence about what Greg had been saying the previous night. About dreams and mushrooms, about realities and their connections. I began to think how unfocussed my own weekend trips were. I was like a tourist, not a traveller. I was just there for a good time, not to make any sense of it. If the experience was to mean anything other than recreation, then there had to be some kind of plan. It couldn't just be dipping in, randomly visiting new realities. It had to be thought through, the way Greg had done. It had to be done with care and preparation, just as you would if you were going to a far-off country. What I had been doing was childlike. Like a child in a fairground I was simply engrossed in the magic of each ride, unable to comprehend the reality of stalls and hucksters. I paddled and thought. I had to address the work thing. I wasn't enjoying what I was doing; it was time for a change.

When I came to the bridge I pulled the canoe ashore and walked to Greg's car which was parked a little way off. There was no one in it, and it was locked. I thought of going looking for them, but I didn't want to leave the canoe unattended. I stood on the bridge and waited. Maybe they had simply gone for a walk, tired of waiting for me. Maybe Greg had deliberately taken the short run and left me the long one to be alone with Jane. I thought about it. A strange idea occurred to me. I didn't mind, and it puzzled me. Jealousy was something I took for granted, something as natural as breathing, and yet I didn't feel it. In fact, I was almost pleased to believe it if it was true. If he had wanted Jane he would never have left her, or she him. I couldn't be jealous of Greg, he was my friend. Such strange thoughts: if I was honest with myself there was even a frisson of excitement in it. For a moment I pictured them in the act, and then I studied the river instead.

There were small trout darting in and out from under the bridge. River weed with long white flowering tresses moved sinuously in the current. Through the shallow brown water the trout were hard to see; only when they moved did the eye pick them up. A watery universe, theirs. Shallow horizons. Then they called me. Greg and Jane with their arms full of mushrooms.

'Look! We've found supper.'

Their pleasure was infectious. My brooding thoughts dispersed and Greg and I busied ourselves getting the canoe back on the roof-rack. We got in and set off.

'When are you leaving, Greg?' I asked.

'This evening. It was just a short visit. I have to get back. I'll leave you two off, then I'm off to the airport.'

'I didn't know. I mean, I had no idea you were off today.'

'Seven o'clock flight, a real red-eye.'

We didn't talk of much in the car on the way home. Just banal small talk. Greg made us laugh with his descriptions of the Santa Barbarians, their gurus, their crystals, their re-birthing. Talk about different realities. It all seemed a million miles from mine. It all seemed to boil down to money. They had it there, in abundance. Enough to indulge the flimsiest of whims. They seemed to have so many choices in their lives that choosing became a problem. You needed a guru to tell you how to spend your time and money. Perhaps it's a problem that would be fun to have, I thought. Maybe I should make some money.

After we left off the canoe I asked whose house it was.

'The brother's. Remember? He runs a carpet warehouse now.'

We got back to our house and Greg turned off the engine. He turned around in his seat and looked back at me and smiled.

'Good to see you both again. It's been a while.'

'Four years.'

'I know. I did want to see you both, though. I'm glad you're together. I always thought you two would get it together. It's a reference point for me.'

'Glad to be of service.'

'No, I don't mean it like that. It's just that you two are so much a part of me. I just want to say thanks.'

'For what?'

'Oh, I don't know. Forget it. Just thanks for a good day. I enjoyed it.' He smiled at Jane.

'Look,' he turned to me, 'I don't know if I should say this, but you seem like you're stuck in something you don't like.'

'I suppose that's true.'

'I'm not trying to give you advice or anything, but it's not just the destination – you have to enjoy the ride as well.'

'I know. I've been thinking about it. About what you said last night. Plenty to mull over.'

'Listen, I hope you two aren't going to get into trouble at work over me.' He turned to Jane. 'I'm going into the boutique on my way to the airport to pick up that coat. Do you want me to pass on a message?'

'No thanks.'

He turned to me again.

'Well, so long old buddy. See you the next time.'

'Bye, Greg. And good luck.'

'You too.'

I got out onto the pavement. Jane leaned over to kiss him goodbye. She got out and we stood, waving, as he drove away, one hand raised out of the window.

'Did he just say he'd been to the boutique?'

'He bought a coat the other day. It needed alterations.'

'You didn't tell me.'

'Didn't I? I must have forgot.'

'Forgot to tell me Greg was back from the States?'

'Sorry.' She turned and walked to the front door. She stopped at the door.

'Are you coming in or staying there?'

I followed her in. I didn't pursue it, didn't want to start a fight. Didn't ask about what had happened at the river. Left it all unsaid. Whatever her relationship was with Greg she clearly felt that it was none of my business. I did ask her about the mushrooms they had picked for supper.

'I think I left them in the car.'

Sparassis crispa. The Cauliflower Mushroom.
Large, 8-20 inches diameter.
Cream to nut-brown. Smell pleasant. Fragile.
At base of coniferous trees. Late summer to late autumn.
Edible. Nutty flavoured flesh.

six

I was sure that the reason the mushroom.man had sent me the last piece was because it described his conversion from being a day-tripper to a full-time traveller. The message was clear: if you want to know about psychotropic mushrooms you're going to have to try them. This was definitely not on my agenda in the near or distant future. I felt that somehow he was trying to push me in that direction and it panicked me a little. I didn't want to become his acolyte – I wanted him to be the subject of my research.

Possibly I was imagining it, but I sensed a danger that I was being manipulated – drawn like a fly into a web. I also felt that to continue the dialogue between us I had to change its direction. The computer reference seemed a good starting point, so I asked him to tell me about that. At least computers were real and tangible. If we could stick to topics that were rooted in the reality that I understood then we would be corresponding as equals. Specifically I expressed an interest in machine intelligence, and I asked him if he had more to say on that topic. He replied within the week.

Attn. mushroom.seeker.
Subject: AI.
23 July.

What fascinates me is taking of a piece of silicon and making it think. It's not the technological wizardry of layering millions of transistors by photo-etching onto a thumbnail-size chip; it's the logical arrangement that allows that chip to process information. That's what's clever. I mean, the chip comes from the manufacturer with a simple instruction set and a couple of memory registers, but that's it. Now comes the creation of the higher-level languages.

I like the creation of language. If language not only reflects but also creates reality, then the creation of a computer language is the creation of a computer reality. I believe that. You have to look at the development of computer languages as you would a child learning its native tongue. At first few words have a meaning for the child, but gradually the child begins to string them together and syntax emerges. With that, higher thought processes become possible. It's the same with silicon thought.

All that a silicon chip can do is add one number to another. You make it multiply by making it add sequentially, subtract by negative adding, divide by sequentially negative adding. The instructions you give to perform these tasks are called routines. Then you build up a library of routines that perform more complex arithmetical functions: then they in turn become the building-blocks of the language.

The chip's own instruction set is called a low-level language because you're dealing with the elementary bits. When you've built up a library of routines you can build a command interpreter, in which one instruction can bring into effect many of the primary routines. It's like the beginning of syntax: you can now talk to the chip in a first-generation language rather than talk directly to the chip's own instruction set.

Like building blocks this process continues. Higher-level languages approximate closer and closer to English. The main difference, apart from a smaller vocabulary, is the need for rigorous internal logic – something we don't really expect from normal language. There is a built-in cost to the construction of higher-level languages, and that is loss of efficiency. An instruction in a high-level language is in many ways a crude instrument. It's simpler to use and much quicker than writing your own instruction set from basics; but it's like a bus. It goes close to where you want to go, but never to your door. It's a compromise between ease of use, compactness and precision.

In practical terms what that has meant is that programs have grown in size exponentially. I had a word processor years ago that was 16k of code, including its own character set and screen handling routines. Today there are word processors that take up a thousand times that memory. They are better and easier to use, but the cost has been in memory requirement. Fortunately memory is cheap and abundant.

For a programmer there is a choice: he can fit the language to the task. If you're writing the world's best chess program, then you write it in as low-level a language as you can, in as tight a code as possible. That ensures speed of processing with no time wasted on higher-level interpreters. Operating systems and device drivers work best when written like this. Other tasks benefit from the ease of programming in higher-level languages – database applications, for example, where blistering speed is not the main requirement. If your typing doesn't leave the cursor behind, then the program is fast enough. In the silicon world you match your language to the task.

The parallels between an infant's first steps in language and the growth of computer language are unavoidable. They follow the same route of development. Since human language dictates the patterns of human thought, it's no surprise that the creators of silicon language have followed the same path. But whereas human language turns to self-reflection, as yet silicon has not.

Years ago I got a long letter from Greg detailing his ideas on this. I don't know why he sent it to me, perhaps it was simply an exercise to clarify his own ideas – maybe it was his testament. He wanted to find the silicon equivalent to psychedelics, something that would have the same effect on silicon-based life as psychedelics had on carbon-based life – a catalyst. He was increasingly convinced that there was no answer to be found in programming. Human genetic code has similarities with machine code. Sometimes when you disassemble code to see what someone else has done, you find chunks that serve no purpose. They're left over from previous versions that no one ever got round to cutting out. There are chunks of human genetic code that serve no apparent purpose; they too seem to be leftovers from a previous version, or a version that never got finished.

What's clever about the human code is its compactness. It describes a complex organism right down to the shape of the fingernails in very little space. How it does this seems to be iteration, which leads me to the fractal world.

Some of the greatest discoveries come from people who have crossed inter-disciplinary boundaries. As our world becomes increasingly specialized there's a risk of researchers being so far inside their own woods that they can't see forests anywhere. Benoit Mandelbrot found his inspiration in the world of chaos theory as applied to the weather. Weather doesn't lend itself to projection easily. You may know where a hurricane is now, and what direction and speed it's been heading in for the last eight hours, but that gives little precision in predicting where it'll be in four hours' time. The more you project forward the more tiny influences grow, sometimes enough to change the whole pattern. There had to be a way of encoding this non-linear behaviour mathematically, a way that allowed for pattern and change simultaneously. Fractal geometry was the answer that Mandelbrot found. Here's a bit of Greg's letter from all those years ago.

'I'm sending you a program that generates fractals on

your VDU. You can print them out as well. The basic instruction set that creates the fractal gingerbread man is short; about thirty lines of code. Yet it produces a thing of extraordinary complexity. The fractal has amazing properties: any part can be magnified to disclose even more wonderful landscapes; and yet there is a coherence. Wherever you look, whatever the magnification, there is always a gingerbread man in the pattern somewhere. The fractal universe is self-similar and also infinitely varied. Yet what are these images other than mathematical limits portrayed on a screen? The algorithm that produces this is $n=n^2+c$; it's not complicated, but it produces complexity. By iterating the algorithm millions of times the strange fractal universe comes to life. You put in a seed number, run it through the algorithm, put the result back into the algorithm and run it again. Do this a hundred times and one of two things happen. Either the number gets increasingly larger or smaller, or it tends to a limit. All you do is check what's happening. If it's tending to a limit then paint a dot on the screen white, if not paint it blue. Increment the seed number and do the same for the next point on the screen. That's the process that creates those wonderful images. Modifying the basic algorithm produces ferns of great delicacy, trees, mollusc shells and coastlines. The more you look, the more of our world appears to be made from fractal shapes.

'Is this the secret? Iteration not only in the genetic construction, but also over generations. Every human generation is an iteration of the basic genetic code, another run of the program with a few tiny changes each time. Who knows how many iterations there have been? If we take hominid existence to be about five million years old then there's been a quarter of a million iterations or more. Enough to turn even a small modification into a large effect. Even human history fits nicely into a fractal view of the world. History is both self-similar yet constantly changing: that's a perfect description of a fractal. In this view each one of us is but a dot amongst billions that make the fractal pattern of human history.

'It occurs to me that that's the route I ought to take. Not to try and write some code that can produce self-reflection, but rather a piece of code that can make small modifications to itself depending on its relationship to the environment. Then just like human generations, I let the program write its own offspring, each offspring minutely different from its parent, and then that offspring becomes the parent of the next generation. You see, I don't write anything except God's code – the seed; the rest is iteration over generations. Something may or may not turn up this way, but I've decided that scattering seeds has to be the answer. I'm writing seed programs constantly now, setting them up to start their own program race, monitoring the old and the new for interesting changes. One died, which I find interesting. After two million iterations it had modified its own code so much that it couldn't replicate any more. The last one of that line just sat there, unable to continue or generate new offspring. Isn't that weird? I haven't created life, but I've created programmable death.'

The letter arrived four days after Greg's own death, along with the program that generated fractals. He took his own life shortly after telling me in the letter about his search to create life. I still don't understand why. The news came the day of particularly heavy rains. Jane and I were alone in the house, struggling with leaks. It was a bald message from a woman whose name meant nothing to me – she just said that Greg had committed suicide and that she had found my telephone number in his diary. The rain, the damp, the dull sky and Greg's death. Jane took it badly: she left the next morning.

I spent hours running the fractal program that Greg had sent. The source code was included, so I could alter it as I wished. The fractal gingerbread man gives up its secrets when magnified. You choose an area and magnify it, zooming in tighter and tighter. The area of interest is the boundary between the incremental numbers and those tending to limits. This is where the patterns are, this is where our interest is stimulated; the frontier between two infinities – the incremental one and the limited one. Only a computer could take this raw data and shape it into a visual representation that pleases the human eye. It's a glimpse of a computer-generated world where apparent landscapes and biological forms are no more than numbers displayed on a screen in a shape that we can understand. Fractals are gateways that let us observe a numerical reality. It's a universe in the sense that it has no limits; you can go on magnifying since numbers are infinite. Magnify the gingerbread man's neck several million times and you'll find the valley of the sea-horses, a strangely beautiful landscape made of shapes that resemble them. Wherever you look beauty abounds.

Mandelbrot's classic paper is 'How long is the coast-line of Britain?' The point is that the answer depends on the scale. If you measure a bay, what size inlet in that bay do you include? The smaller the inlets allowable the larger the measurement becomes, although it will tend to a limit. Coastlines are a good example of fractals. They, too, are self-similar. Small inlets look much like large bays; only the scale changes. Like fractals they are a combination of difference and self-similarity. It's like standing on a strange and infinitely large carpet. There appears to be a pattern, but as you move over it the pattern changes, slowly, imperceptibly. When it has become very different, there, imbedded in the pattern, is a smaller-scale version of the original pattern. An eternally shifting design of difference and similarity.

A fractal isn't simply an oddity that provides a pretty picture on a screen, it has real uses. To create a virtual-reality world you have to generate backgrounds – that is, a universe in which to set the artificial reality. The easiest way to do this, keeping the instruction set small, is to create the backgrounds from fractal algorithms on the fly. Complex backgrounds can be built up from a short set of instructions. This more than anything else is the fractal lesson. Complexity can be generated from simplicity by iterating a simple formula. It's a thought that haunts me every time I look at a fern; it's so obviously fractal-generated. The secret to complex life forms is iteration of simple rules that allow for tiny changes on each iteration. Greg was right to scatter his program seeds and let them replicate themselves; it's a way close in form to the life that surrounds us.

Virtual reality is an interesting prospect. You've got the apparent reality without the intelligence. You provide the intelligence in a reality not of your making. The range of realities available are limited only by the programmer's imagination. You move around in a reality of someone else's making. When the world of virtual reality becomes interactive, then you have a reality not far removed from dreams. Every whim, every wanderlust, every fantasy becomes possible. It is also a sanitized world where danger doesn't exist. No germs, no viruses, no sabre-toothed tigers – at least, not real ones. It's conceivable that all the technology to create a virtual reality could be put into an exoskeleton that you could wear, like a suit of armour. Inside the shell you could inhabit the world of your choice and the time of your choice.

For the moment the worlds of virtual reality are the product of human imagination. But suppose control of the artificial reality were to be handed over to a machine intelligence. What kind of reality would it create for us? Virtual reality then becomes a gateway that allows us access to worlds not of human imagining. What strange vistas might open up, surreal landscapes where nothing is familiar, where nothing has relevance to our baggage of experience. It's possible that something so different, so alien, would cause us some kind of sensory overload. With nothing of our past experience to relate to we may find ourselves so adrift that we would simply switch off, unable to cope.

I try to imagine parallels here with mushroom realities. In many ways these realities seem closer to the dream state than the reality of the everyday. The difference seems to be in the brain's responses to stimuli. Psilocybin, like all the indole group of psychedelics, changes the nature of the chemical bath that surrounds our neurons, and hence the responses of the brain's synapses. The neural networks and pathways are affected: new connections become possible, new paths through the nexus are created. Barriers that separate the visual from the auditory, the olfactory from the tactile, become permeable. New matrices of thought are possible and existent. In dreams space and linear time cease to exist. What we call logical thought stops. Possibly it is all a function of the loss of linearity. For most people the dream state is the only state of altered consciousness that they deal with. Yet despite its universality it remains largely unexplored, unmapped. Somewhere on our journey towards a silicon world the knowledge of the sorcerers has been lost. The dream maps are slowly fading away, buried beneath our technology.

The universe of the sorcerer – the shaman world – has never disappeared, it's only been eclipsed. In many parts of the globe it's the dominant reality. Monotheism and technology are its antithesis. In the western world of high technology the myths that remain part of our heritage are no longer relevant to our lives. To us they are simply stories. But back then, in that pantheistic world, they described reality fully, exactly, and relevantly. Somewhere in our genetic inheritance these myths remain, or at least the dark shapes that created them do. On inward journeys these atavistic shades can be found; the ogres and the gods – banished by rationalism but surviving still, waiting like Pandora's box to be opened and unleashed once more.

I don't find that a worry. On an evolutionary scale our rational, technological world is a blink of the eye. More of our genetic code exists to deal with the shaman's world than with the world of developed economies. The sense of wonder, of belonging, that the mushroom engenders is not accidental. The mushroom is only a trigger; unleashing the suppressed racial memories, letting us into the dream-time once more. It is feared more than anything else, more than nuclear war. The whole controlling thrust of western society is geared toward keeping the dream-time at bay. I can only speculate why this should be so. Maybe because self-exploration rather than watching television makes society harder to control. Perhaps. The fear of toadstools, too, must have its roots in the witch-hunts of the fifteenth century. What is witchcraft if not the return to pre-monotheistic earth-worship? Witchcraft was never the antithesis to Christianity: it existed in its own right and predated monotheism. It's the tail end of the Gaia tradition; the communion with nature. Thrusting, aggressive, male monotheism has never completely replaced the female, pantheistic earth-worship of the dream-time.

I'm not a proselyte, never was. I have no urge to knock on doors and say 'you're wrong, I'm right, listen to me'. But I do want to say that although I tread a different path, I'm not a threat. I ask for no one to follow me. I'm happy to travel alone on the less trodden path. Why should I and my fellow-travellers be feared and even persecuted? Is my madness any less coherent than anyone else's? Is it infectious? I can start no wars, create no economic chaos; I move in an internal world, in a matrix far from society's hub.

Even so, our worlds appear to be approaching one another. The global village is growing, the information superhighway has more and more connections. This is a reality based on a network; you don't touch, see or feel, but you communicate. Soon even this will change. You'll be able to virtually see, touch and smell on the Internet. When I plug into my exoskeleton I'll be able to touch you in yours through the ether. Technology will bring us to where I am now. I can do that: reach out and touch through the ether, fly where the imagination soars. Yet my route there is feared and proscribed – while the other route is backed by stocks and shares. It makes no sense to me.

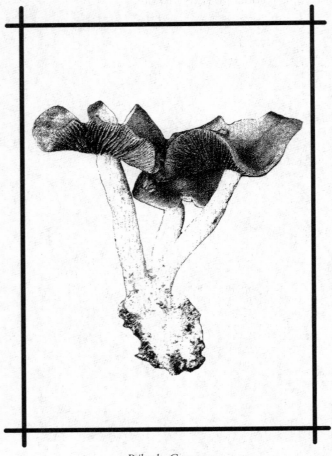

Psilocybe Cyanescens.
Small to medium size. Cap 1-2 inches. In clusters.
Russet drying to dull cream.
Quite rare, grows on rotting debris. Late autumn to early winter. Hallucinogenic.

seven

It occurred to me that even computers ended up relating to mushrooms in the mushroom.man's world. I'd followed the instructions he'd sent me and downloaded the program for generating fractals from the net. It was fascinating, and absorbed me totally for hours at a time. The fractal universe is astounding in its complexity and beauty, but the practical result of using it was that I replaced my monochrome monitor with a large colour one capable of high-definition graphics. What was already a visual delight in black and white became mind-boggling in 64k colour. It became the first practical result of my interaction with the mushroom.man, and I was intensely grateful for it.

I became once more determined to find out from him all that I could about his actual experiences with mushrooms. I put aside whatever reservations I had had about being drawn unwillingly into his world. After all, my contact with the mushroom.man was not physical so there was no possibility of coercion. All we could exchange were ideas, and even they were not part of a contemporaneous dialogue. There was always time to analyse whatever he'd sent me before there was a need to reply. That was an aspect of this kind of electronic communication that I liked: it suited my temperament. There was never a need to answer or react at once as there is in a face-to-face conversation. Like a game of postal chess you could sit and think, formulate a response and then communicate it.

Even though I occasionally felt a frisson of danger in the contact with some of his ideas, the method of communication seemed to hold some defence for me by virtue of its inherent properties — the time-lag, the distance, the anonymity. It offered me protection. And I took heart from his declaration that he was no proselyte — he was not looking for disciples.

I sent him this e-mail:

Attn. mushroom.man.
Subject: the usual.
26 July.

You've given me glimpses of your world and how you see it. But what I still haven't grasped is how mushrooms change your perceptions. Maybe what I should be asking is 'what's it like to go tripping?' I do understand the physiological processes, but as you say, that's understanding form but not content. It's something I'd like to understand a little better; I can't help feeling that if I were to have a better grasp of it, much of what you have written would make more sense to me. Forgive me for making the same plea over and over again, but tell me more.

Along with his reply, which came a few days later, came instructions as to where to find an updated version of the fractal program and how to download it into my own computer.

Attn. mushroom.seeker.
Subject: alternate realities.
1 August.

I've said it before and I'll repeat it again; you can't use words to describe the non-verbal. Still, you keep asking so I'm sending you a description of alternate realities. Who knows? It may even make sense to you:

I felt tired. I sat down in my armchair and fell asleep. When I woke up I was lying by the river bank, which was bathed in a pinkish light. I looked at the sky. It was a uniform light green, which contrasted oddly with the suffused light around me. It felt warm and comfortable; a gentle breeze rustled the leaves and ruffled the surface of the river, which appeared to be hardly flowing. I was surprised to notice that I had no shoes on, no socks, no shirt, and that I was wearing what seemed to be calico trousers with a fly-flap like sailors' bell-bottoms. I stood and found that the pebbles of the river bank were soft and giving underfoot, as though made of rubber.

I became aware that there was no bird-song. There was an almost total silence; only the wind in trees made a sound. The river looked almost like a lake, glass-surfaced, quiet, deep. I swam, gingerly at first but with growing enthusiasm. The water was warm and very clear. With my face in the water I could see the bottom, the stones, the river weed. Four trout swam past lazily, browsing occasionally on the weed, rummaging in the gritty sand between the stones. There was no current, and I floated, arms and legs akimbo. I watched the trout, who seemed unaware of my presence. They moved slowly, edging toward a large bank of weed. As they approached there was a flash of silver. A large pike darted out from the weed cover and took a trout cross-ways in his bill. While the trout's tail flailed the pike appeared to stare at me, unblinkingly. The three other trout moved on unhurriedly, unconcerned, while the pike remained motionless. I could hear the beat of the trout's flapping tail, rhythmically keeping time to its death rattle. Slowly the flapping stopped, the trout's mouth gaped open in a bizarre grin. The pike's pectoral fins twitched, then started a slow beat. The fins were almost transparent, big, lazy, floppy things like an elephant's ears. The pike's broad, flat, duck-bill shone with a brown lustre; tiny clouds of blood rose from the trout where the pike's teeth had penetrated the scales. They hung in the water, growing slowly. Idly the pike opened its jaws once or twice, turning the trout round, head towards its gullet. A gulp, and the trout was gone. I watched as a lump moved through the pike's body until it came to rest in the belly. Another sudden flurry and the pike was gone.

I was breathing easily and felt carefully around my neck. I could feel my gills opening and closing in time with my breath. I looked at my hands, unsurprised to see skin webbing between the fingers. I moved away from the weed bed and swam to deeper water. The bottom was free of weed – perhaps thirty or forty feet deep. I swam to the bottom. A movement behind a boulder caught my eye. Two crayfish were engaged in a strange dance, hopping on their tails like fleas. They were locked together by their claws; dust rose in clouds with every hop. I sat on the river bed, motionless, engrossed in their dance. I could hear the creaks of their tails as the segments bent and straightened.

A school of minnows passed me by, turning and darting simultaneously, as though directed by a single will. A round stone, well smoothed by the water, lay by my feet. I turned it over to find the terrifying ugliness of a crane fly larva, startled by exposure. It startled us both, that unexpected meeting. I was gulping in water, shocked by its unremitting ugliness and closeness. Horrid things that live under stones, hiding their shame: covert horrors that are the stuff of nightmare.

It occurred to me that if this was a dream, then I could do what I wanted; perhaps, as Greg once explained, I could control the dream. I decided to swim fast for the surface and emerge flying. I broke the surface, I willed for flight, but none came. I swam to the shore and lay on the grassy verge. In the light green sky bright stars flickered, making constellations that I had never seen. An unfamiliar sky; wrong colour; stars by day. I turned and lay on my front. The grass was soft, but was made of fibre. Between the blades there were psilocybin mushrooms growing: I picked and ate all that were in reach. I watched a fog roll down the river valley, billowing like a cloud, cascading in slow motion, filling the space between the trees.

I was enveloped in a warm, moist blanket. I could see clearly the tiny droplets that made the mist – sparkling, bright droplets that shimmered, danced in agitation. It caressed me like a bath, I could feel it in my lungs. When I exhaled my breath was visible, blue against the white mist. I became aware of the mist's noise; a kind of gentle thunder, like a far-away storm. It moved past me, the tiny droplets hopping and bouncing, crashing into one another in the haste of their Brownian motion.

When it had passed I was standing on a high crag, looking at a valley that stretched out below me into a hazy horizon. A loud caw made me turn. Perhaps twenty feet from me a large raptor, maybe an eagle, was in a nest. It was trampling the nest bottom, moving round and round in circles inside the eyrie. I noticed that its mate was circling above, riding a thermal. Gradually it became harder to see as its helical path took it higher into the light green sky.

I was sure now that I was dreaming. There was no logic to my movements; only dream-time logic. I had no idea where this valley was, I'd never seen it before. It was big, stretching into the distance, covered in what seemed to be fields. I stared at my hands; I pinched one. I saw the red welt of the pinch form. I pinched again. I heard a voice calling me. It was Jane.

'What are you doing here?' she asked as she walked up to me.

'I'm not sure. I was watching the eagle.'

'You shouldn't be here.'

'Why did you leave me?'

'I didn't. You left me. You were never with me. You never made me part of your life.'

'That's not true. I loved you. I think I still do.'

She sat down on the craggy outcrop and scanned the horizon. She was silent and still. I watched her; her long black hair moved in the occasional breeze, her shoulders imperceptibly rising and falling with breath.

She turned.

'You shouldn't be here, you know.'

'Where's here?'

She laughed and pointed behind me. I saw my house between the trees. When I turned she was gone. There was a large henge in the field in front of the house made of huge, irregular granite boulders. In the centre was a trilith shaped like an altar. A man sat on its lip. When he turned to me, it was Greg.

'Greg?'

'Of course.'

I stopped. Greg couldn't be here. I shook my head. He watched me for a moment, then laughed. His mouth was wide open and I saw that his teeth were black and rotting. Two front ones were missing.

'Greg?'

'What?'

'Are you really here?'

'Of course. You called me.'

'Where are we?'

'You called me here. You ought to know.'

'But I don't. Jane was here too. I just saw her.'

'Of course you did. What do you want?'

'I want to know where I am.'

'Knowing where you are is a good start.'

He jumped down from the rock and dusted the seat of his pants. He looked about.

'Some sort of megalithic lunar observatory, I suppose.'

'What is?'

'This is. It's where you are.' He smiled. His teeth disturbed me.

'I don't understand. I thought you were dead. I thought Jane was in London. That isn't my house. There's no stone circle outside my house.'

'That's your house there.'

'I'm lost, I think. I was sitting in my house, in the armchair, I was thinking. Maybe I fell asleep. If this is a dream then I'm probably sitting in the armchair in there.'

'Not unless you can be in two places at once.'

'What?'

'Easy. If you're here, you can't be there.'

I was bewildered. I remembered an old man had told me once that if the fairies bewitch you in a field you'll never find the gate. The only way to break the spell is to take your coat off, turn it inside out and put it on again. But I was still wearing only trousers. A wave of panic seized me and I vomited. The bitter taste of bile was lodged in my throat. Greg led me to the house.

Inside was familiar, but not exactly as I knew it. It was as if the house was someone else's memory of my house. Mostly right, but with details missing or wrong. There was a bronze horse on the window ledge that I'd never seen before. The walls weren't the right colour. Greg lit a fire in the grate. The wood crackled and spat. He sat down on the sofa and looked at me.

'Why did you call me here?'

'I didn't. I don't think I did. I don't know what's happening. This makes no sense. I don't think this is my house. It just looks like it.'

'It's your house, old buddy. Yours and Jane's.'

'No, Jane's gone. She doesn't live with me any more.'

'Well that looks like Jane to me coming up the path.'

He pointed through the window. Jane was walking toward the house with some cut flowers in her hand. She saw me in the window and waved. I turned to Greg.

'I don't understand.'

'What's to understand?'

The door opened and Jane walked in. She found a vase, a strange blue glass one, and put the flowers in.

'There.' She stood back and admired them. 'Don't they look nice?'

'They're beautiful,' said Greg.

Jane sat down on the sofa next to Greg. They were both facing me, like a jury in judgement. Jane watched me carefully for a moment.

'You don't look very well,' she said.

'I'm fine. I'm well. I'm just a bit tired. A bit tired, that's all. I saw a pike today. I ate some mushrooms. Maybe that's it. I ate some mushrooms. I remember now, by the river. They were growing in the grass. But it wasn't grass. Maybe I imagined it. I don't know. I thought I'd fallen asleep.'

'You don't look well to me, either,' said Greg. 'You look sick.'

At this Greg and Jane were convulsed with giggles. I noticed Greg's teeth again. I could feel my stomach knotting. I opened a window and took deep breaths. I could hear them behind me, laughing. The sky still had that pale green colour. It was light, but there was no sign of a sun; no source for the brightness. Suddenly I felt very cold. There were goose pimples on my arms – the hairs were standing on end.

'I'm going to put on a sweater,' I said.

'Good idea.' They broke into laughter again.

My bedroom was completely unfamiliar. The thought occurred to me again that this was someone else's idea of where I lived.

Someone who didn't really know what the bedroom looked like. Couldn't be Jane. Maybe this was Greg's idea, Greg's reality. That made sense. This was Greg's reality; how he remembered our house; how he remembered us. He couldn't know that Jane had left me – she didn't leave till after he was dead. The two things came together – they were connected. I found a pullover on the bed and put it on. It wasn't mine. I felt more comfortable, warmer, less confused. This was not my reality.

I walked back into the sitting room. Greg was standing with his back to the fire, Jane was still sitting on the sofa. I decided to ask him.

'Is this how you remember us?'

'This is how I see you.'

'Together?'

'The three of us together.'

I looked at Jane. I wanted to know if this was the Jane of my memories or his. I tried to remember if any of her things were in the bedroom. Clothes, or perfume, or anything. I asked her.

'Is this where we live?'

'It's where I live. My house. That's my pullover you're wearing.'

'You live in London. You have children.'

'I live here. I told you outside, I'm not sure you should be here.'

'Where should I be?'

'I don't know – it's just that I don't think you should be here now. Not now.'

I looked at my wrist, hoping to see my watch. It wasn't there. I had no idea what time it was, what date it was. I was sure that if I knew that, then I could make sense of it all.

Greg went to the door. He beckoned me to follow. I walked out behind him and we were standing on the crag overlooking the valley. The eagle and its nest were gone. It was getting dark.

'Look there.' Greg pointed to the lights of a sprawling city that I hadn't seen the last time. 'That's where I live. I come up here to get away from it all, to get a perspective. There are eagles up here.'

'I know.'

'Down there is where I work. Up here is where I think. I keep the two things separate. Thinking and working. Yin and Yang. Separate, but entwined. The work is very demanding, you have no idea.'

'I think I might.'

'It's not like college. There's a pressure that's hard to explain. A pressure to get results, thousands of tiny goals that are set and then have to be reached. None of any consequence individually, but daunting because of their number, their continuous, unrelenting presence. There's a pressure to have new ideas, to find new ways of seeing problems. It's a vortex, old buddy. The more ideas you have, the more are demanded of you. It becomes expected, it becomes the norm. The pressure to create.'

'Do you love Jane?'

'What?'

'Do you love her?'

'You weren't listening, were you?'

'I just want to know did you love her, I mean, do you love her?'

'Of course I love her. She was my first love – probably the only real love of my life.'

'Why did you leave her?'

'Is that why you called me? Why you brought me here? Is that what you wanted to know?'

'I suppose it must be. I've never known the answer. Never talked about it before.'

'You're something else, old buddy. Of all the things you need answers to, that's what you want to ask me?'

'Yes.'

'This isn't easy. But I'll tell you the truth. You remember the night in the van?'

'Yes.'

'I felt that I'd sullied her somehow. I felt guilty. I couldn't look her in the eye any more, so I knew it was hopeless. Anyway, I think she liked you.'

'Liked me.'

'Loved. You know what I mean.'

'Do you remember when we went canoeing?

'Of course.'

'You were in the woods with her, picking mushrooms.'

'Yes.'

'Did you make love to her?'

'What kind of question is that?'

'Did you?'

'No. I told her what I've just told you. I told her that I'd always loved her and always would. Perhaps distance, time and guilt built it up into something unrealistic, something unreal. But it's how I feel. You know, you're a lucky man, old buddy, not many people ever find straight answers to their questions.'

'I know.'

'Pity the questions were so stupid.'

The city lights shimmered in the increasing darkness. I could hear the cricket song gathering momentum. Cars moved in an endless procession up and down the highways that cut across the valley floor.

'Greg?'

'Yes.'

'Is this real?'

'What?'

'The valley. The city. You.'

'If you perceive it, then it's real. Reality is about perception. You want to know about objective realities, and I'll tell you. Sit still and listen. Reality is the product of intelligence. Your intelligence creates the reality you perceive; creates it out of sensory stimuli. Similar intelligences create similar realities, so there are common points of reference. You can call that objective reality if you like. But a different intelligence will not inhabit the same reality as you, there will be few if any points of common reference. I can conceive of a machine intelligence that senses its environment like you do, that can react to it and even modify it. But I'm sure whatever reality exists for machine intelligence, it's very different from that of biological intelligence.'

'Can you do it? Create intelligence?'

'All depends on what you mean by intelligence, doesn't it?'

'I feel tired.'

'I know.'

'I miss you, Greg. I'm sorry we didn't have more time with one another. We could have grown old together.'

'You can see me anytime you want.'

'How?'

'All you have to do is call.'

I heard Jane calling for Greg. He stood up.

'I have to go now, old buddy. See you.'

He walked away and a rush of sadness engulfed me. Sadness for how things were; how they could have been. I missed him, I missed Jane. I cried the self-indulgent tears of a man pleased with his sorrow. Had she ever loved me?

I watched the city lights through eyes filled with salty tears, enjoying the prickling sensation in my eyelids. The crickets were loud now, their song coming in waves, washing over me like a lullaby. I fought sleep – I was scared of where I might wake up. But I couldn't move. A heavy lethargy had overtaken me, and I knew that I couldn't leave this spot. There was soft grass on the crag, welcoming. I lay back and stared at the sky, black now, with the same strange constellations. I saw a spider made of stars, a hand, a face. I think I slept.

I woke up on the river bank in daylight, cold and stiff. Stones had been pressing into my back; I felt bruised and sore. I was wearing my own clothes, but they were damp with the fallen dew. My watch said seven o'clock, the sun was in the east – it was morning.

I walked back to my house. The lights were on and the front door was wide open. The remains of a fire glowed in the hearth. The dog stretched, yawned, and wagged its tail. I was home, this was my house.

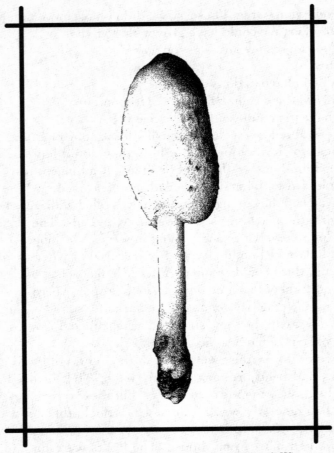

Coprinus comatus. The Shaggy Ink Cap or Lawyer's Wig.
4-6 inches high. In family groups.
White auto-digesting to black.
Common on paths and roadsides. Late summer to autumn.
Edible while white, good for soup. Once used for ink.

eight

I was beginning, I thought, to have a clearer idea of who the mush-room.man was. I began preparing a paper on the effects of long-term use of psychedelics, using the mushroom.man as my reference. Although the life he described was essentially simple and rural, it included computers, so there was some element of sophistication. If what he was sending me was an accurate description of his way of life then it seemed that he still retained an ability to deal effectively with daily life. This is something that long-term users of heroin, for example, are incapable of for the most part.

He was obviously well educated and had evolved ideas about reality that were quirky, but plausible. Not all of them made much sense to me, some seemed to be the ramblings of a mind damaged by chemical inges-tion. Still, the ideas were interesting from a clinical point of view. I was keen to make an impression on my department and I felt that this kind of field research might well impress my colleagues.

I'd been pressing him recently for his thoughts on what he called his psychic travels. Specifically I wanted to know if there was a coherent phi-losophy underpinning his use of psychedelics. By this stage I had done a lot of research on the subject in the university library. There was a large body of work done in the sixties on psychedelics, and LSD in particular, which I read assiduously. Most of it concerned the clinical use of LSD in psychiatry as a tool for analysis, but one report caught my eye as being of relevance. It concerned the effects of cannabis on jazz musicians. Once the mushroom.man had written that his use of cannabis was to enhance his enjoyment of music. The study that I had found, by E. G. Williams *in the* US Public Health Report, *was clear in its conclusions. Despite the claims of jazz musicians that the drug was enhancing their music, the laboratory tests showed that their ability to identify a single note or assess its duration was impaired. It seemed fairly conclusive to me.*

I sent him the relevant extracts from this report and asked for his comments. I think that this was one of the very few times he ever gave me a specific reply to a specific question. His response seemed almost angry. I must be a fool, he wrote, if I thought that making music or enjoying it had anything to do with being able to name the notes. Is this what makes the music of Schubert touch the soul, being able to name the notes? In a Pythagorean universe, numbers underpin everything including the structure of the diatonic scale, but how can understanding the numbers explain the effect on our emotions? Whoever this E. G. Williams is, he has a weird idea of what music is or how to assess its quality.

As an argument it sidestepped the core issue of impairment of ability, but I pressed it no further. Instead I took up the Pythagorean theme of numbers being the basis of all things in our universe. Certainly statistical analysis formed a major part of my work — it was a tool I could scarcely do without when dealing with raw data. But I was curious to know what part numbers played in his world. Eventually he sent me this.

Attn. mushroom.seeker.
Subject: Mathematics and the shaman universe.
13 August.

In all the years that I lived with Jane I'd never been able to talk to her about mathematics. A glazed look would come into her eye; my enthusiasm was never infectious. She refused to accept that it could have any relevance to her life. She'd say, 'I don't need to know any of that.' I'd talk about classical Greek architecture, so bound up with the irrational number phi – the golden ratio. How mathematics and form were linked, how the underlying discipline made the shapes pleasing to the eye. I've always believed that knowledge of any kind is a useful tool, that it can be used not only to understand, but to create. If the early geometers hadn't discovered the properties of a 3,4,5 triangle they'd never have got a square base to the pyramids.

I don't think that there's anything ethereal about mathematics. It's a branch of learning with very real, tangible products. It can also describe the universe well. If that weren't true you couldn't send an unmanned spacecraft to Mars. As a description of our universe it works; every lunar landing was a proof. The trouble is, of course, extracting the ideas from the arcane figures and notations. Some ideas are complex and incomprehensible, others so beautifully simple and elegant that they startle. I've never believed that these ideas should be left as the preserve of mathematicians, they're too good not to steal.

We were all taught a mechanistic view of physics. Things worked by laws that were demonstrable and repeatable. You could reduce the movement of celestial bodies or the swing of a pendulum to an elegant set of simultaneous equations. What was happening was that to reduce the observed phenomena to neat and tidy equations you had to leave bits out, or they didn't work. The swing of a pendulum works in a mathematical model as long as you don't include a three-dimensional wobble. The pendulum has to swing in a two-dimensional plane. Real pendulums don't do that, of course. To make a mathematical model of a real pendulum's swing requires horrendous equations – unless we address the problem differently. If you use fuzzy logic – logic that allows for wobbles – you get a close approximation to observed phenomena. It's good at describing rules for a quantum universe. In fact there's nothing fuzzy about the logic, it's the rules that are fuzzy: that is, they're more like English than maths. You can tell a room heater 'if it gets a bit colder turn up the heat a little'. That's a lot closer to the kind of logic we use daily than pure mathematics. In a way it's like developing a meta-language of logic from functions – rather like a high-level computer language constructed from binary logic bits.

I remember once sitting in the woods and deciding to mark the passage of time by the swaying of a branch in the wind. The wilder the wind the faster the passage of time; the more gentle, the slower time passed. Time was matched to my sense of being, not to a quartz crystal. In this part of the country an acre of land used to be enough land on which to pasture a cow. This was fuzzy logic at its best: on poor land the acre was large, on good land it was smaller. The measurement was fuzzy, but the information was precise. If you bought an acre, you knew you'd bought enough land to pasture a cow, and therefore it was easy to work out your return from the money invested. The old acre was a measurement that included within it years of observation of the land and the climate; it was matched specifically to the area it measured. When that method of measurement was lost, so was all the information that went with it. Yet it remains in folk memory as an example of how the world was once viewed, before the rigorous homogeneity of the modern state took hold.

Discoveries in mathematics are no different in their effects than discoveries in other disciplines. If they fit into the existing schema they present no problems and are readily accepted. If something is discovered that doesn't fit, that refuses to conform with the currently accepted wisdom, then it tends to be shelved and ignored. Only when the shelf is bulging with things that don't fit the current theory does it become time to change the theory. The strange functions that defied differentiation; functions that had singularities; mathematical oddities for half a century – were precisely those that led Mandelbrot to his fractal geometry and by analogy to chaos theory as well. He found a new way of ordering the data that made sense of what had been regarded as curiosities. It is not a binary universe; chaos and order are not the only alternatives. There is a boundary area between the two that exhibits a little of both states. This is where the fractal universe lives. The world and its physics are fuzzy; our universe is lumpy. Order and exactness are what we want to find, not what's there.

Thinkers in the Aristotelian school find this way of looking at things anathema. Fuzzy and lumpy are exactly the epithets that they are at pains to eradicate from their world view. And there is no doubt that the mechanistic view of the universe has been successful: it has brought us to the technologically wondrous world that we now inhabit. Computers are the logical result of addressing the universe linearly. But it does seem that somewhere on the journey from Aristotle to here we lost sight of some other part of ourselves, the part that deals not in logic and equations but in perceptions and dreams. I sense a shamanistic revival; a groundswell of ill-defined discontent seems to be taking a gradual form, a shape that expresses itself in the non-material spheres. Earth magic, Buddhism, witchcraft, re-birthing, druidism – all these point in a similar direction. There is a sense that we have explored one road well; so well that it has been to the detriment of others.

All the time I was living with Jane many ideas began to form, loosely at first, but then with gathering clarity. It was frustrating not to be able to bounce them off Jane, check them out against her feedback. It's hard to think in a vacuum, especially if you doubt your own sanity at the same time.

Reading was the only route available to me to keep some kind of tab on where my thoughts were leading. Bibliographies of sources were the only pointers I had to other ways of thinking, and getting books not in the mainstream of publishing was hard. Still, my bookshelves are a monument to the cabala of mushrooms. There is an enormous jumble of information on ethnopharmacology, from the scholarly to the frankly bizarre. Between these extremes there does seem to be some common ground, some agreement. That the hallucinogenic experience has had a large and quantifiable effect on western societies and thought is clear enough. Myths and legends can be interpreted with little difficulty as parables, attempts to give an insight into worlds where words have little meaning. All through recorded history there are descriptions of rites and mysteries that appear to have mushrooms at the heart of them. Men and mushrooms have a long and entwined history.

No matter how you try, the problem is still the same one. Explaining a world where words have no meaning, to a world where words are the only meaning, has inherent paradoxes. It can't be confronted directly, only obliquely; hence the myths, parables and legends. The lack of clarity is not only because of the difficulty of describing the indescribable, but also because over many centuries the secret rites and mysteries were feared and proscribed. Circumlocution was often the only way to pass on information without persecution.

Essentially that is still the case. The modern *Malleus Malefecorum* is the global war on drugs – demonology has simply changed its target. Unfortunately the target has been made large and amorphous. Heroin- and cocaine-induced crime and sociological disintegration have been lumped together with mushrooms, tryptamines and indoles. Yet the effect of hallucinogens is to break habits of behaviour and thought; quite the contrary of the white powders. Demonizing drugs has led us to throw away a real tool for self-awareness. Oversimplification has produced modern mantras repeated in all of our media. *Television good, drugs bad.* Ignorance and repression of the unknown have always been universal currencies.

I keep coming up against an intellectual wall. Moments of intuition, moments of epiphany, never become moments of elation. The dampening factor is arrogance. It's a wall I find hard to get past. Every time an apparent insight comes, a voice within says 'Don't be so arrogant. Why should you have discovered something no one else has?' The only response I've ever been able to find is that it's perhaps because I was looking where few others have explored. That allows me to believe in the validity of an insight while retaining an intellectual modesty. Every virgin territory has discoveries waiting to be made by even the least perceptive. Obviously it follows that the better explored the territory, the harder new discoveries are to make.

The other major doubt is the one that says, 'If this way of life is so fulfilling, why are you permanently poor and alone?' That's easier to deal with than the first, because loneliness and discomfort are simply a product of exploration. If I had surrounded myself with comforts and friends then there would be no solitude, and with no solitude no exploration. Although easily answered it is none the less a recurring doubt. Sometimes when I sit in the damp and cold surrounded by seventeenth-century technology I wonder about the wisdom of my choices. They were never intended to be so, but they can look obdurately wilful at times.

To me, however, they seem real choices. Not the choices that are fobbed off on us by advertisers and industry whose battle cry of 'freedom to choose' means nothing more than a choice of breakfast cereals. Free will has been redefined; its only application is in the world of consumerism. You are free to choose the car of your choice, the house of your choice, the pension plan of your choice, but there is an underlying criterion for this freedom: purchase. The only freedom on offer in a consumer-led society is the freedom to spend.

Like everyone else I often ask myself, 'Where do I go from here?' There has to be a point to it, a purpose, a goal where the journey ends. There is something unsatisfying about the idea of a life-long search that ends with nothing to report. *Whizz. What was that? Your life, pal. Anything to report? No, not really.* Depressing thought. So there has to be a rationale. It means having to define some of my ramblings as purposeful journeys. It means investing banal thoughts with deeper meanings. Re-defining enforced choices as acts of will. Obviously I'm aware of these tendencies and try to curtail them, but some get past me. It's a constant struggle.

Is it worth it? Although I have doubts, I suppose I must believe the answer is yes. I wouldn't be here otherwise. In the final analysis we measure our lives by the pleasure received against the pain received. I may have discomfort, but there is little if any pain. And pleasures are there too. If I'm to be specific, then the pleasures are all of the same kind; pleasures found by being part of the natural world. The splash of a kingfisher, the majesty of a twelve-point stag, the fruiting of a mushroom. Pleasure in being part of the grander scheme of things; those rare moments when you feel a sense of belonging as opposed to alienation. And pleasure too in those moments of insight.

I worry that any social skills I may have had are withering from lack of use. In company I still feel as I always did, still believe myself to be normal and average, but increasingly I'm aware that people are treating me differently. As though I'm some kind of alien species. It's nothing tangible; I can't put my finger on any specifics, it's just a feeling. It might be something as simple as my appearance; maybe I'm beginning to look like the wild man of the mountains. I think that's what happens. Gradually, imperceptibly, you begin to assume the camouflage that best fits your surroundings. Look at me, I'm dressed entirely in greens and browns. There's a bit of the chameleon in us all.

If it wasn't for the changing seasons my days would have a stifling monotony. The seasons at least change the back-drop against which I act. They create their own set of daily routines and actions, they point to the passing of time. And that's another worry of mine, getting older and no wiser. I could be wiser, if only I could remember some of the things I've learned. Time passes unobtrusively here, it sneaks past you like a rat in the dark. If time is measured by movement, then it's no surprise you don't spot its passing here. Nothing changes, nothing moves.

Time is one of the things that changes from world to world. Outside the daily world of consciousness it doesn't have the same driving urgency. The advances in time-keeping create paradoxes of their own. A stopped clock is right twice a day; one that loses only a hundredth of a second a day is right once every 12,000 years. Once you start down the Aristotelian path of science and dissection you have to go to ridiculous extremes to get back to where you were before you started. I sometimes wonder whether I need a watch or not, or even a calendar. I can't think of anything that I do that requires that kind of temporal precision.

Diversity is increasingly giving way to monoculture. Global networks of television, communications and computers are slowly homogenizing our world. There are no parts of the planet left that a lone wanderer can explore. Maybe that's the attraction of inner space, it's accessible to everyone and largely unexplored. A place that appeals to the frontiersman; a place with no regulations, no signposts, no roads. It's the antithesis of the urban world.

As political and economic power is increasingly centralized, so the ideals and the philosophies of the urban mind have begun to dominate. Its urge to put systems in place, to set everything in concrete, to pass laws that ultimately prevent the individual from taking responsibility for his own life, is making existence on the frontiers harder to sustain. Living outside the system is getting harder. As government databases grow and communications get faster and more efficient, the urban net is ever more encompassing. More and more the countryside is perceived and regulated as a theme-park for the urban visitor. The frontier is losing its wildness and its inhabitants their freedom.

How far has the urban mind moved from the land when it deems it intelligent to make a plant illegal? Mutter what you like about biodiversity and animal rights, but where is the sense in outlawing a plant? How does an organism that has existed longer than the human race become unlawful? I'm not an anarchist; I believe in laws and a society that is regulated to ensure the greater good but I'm sure that the regulatory urge has been given too free a rein.

Until things change the only true freedom to be found is

in inner space. Here dreams and imagination make the fabric that defines it, and by their nature they are both boundless. There are no limits in this space; that is both its attraction and its drawback. Complete freedom means there is freedom to make bad or unwise choices, freedom to go to places where the sensible wouldn't venture, freedom to express both the good and the bad in our souls. The only repercussions to these choices, both good and bad, are from the traveller's own sense of self-discipline. It's what Carlos Castaneda called the warrior's path, where the individual makes the rules and lives by them, taking responsibility for his actions and their effects. I have a need to make my own decisions, to find my own route to knowledge.

Just what knowledge is can be hard to pin down. It's the result of exploration either of ideas or of physical space. It can be immediate in its application like the knowledge of fire, or it can remain intangible like knowledge of the cosmos. We seek it because knowledge is power, and sometimes it converts to money. If you were a druid and could use your henge to predict eclipses, you had power over your society. You could make an eclipse the response of the gods to your society's careless treatment of its priests. When Arab traders learnt that the stars Phad and Dubhe pointed to Polaris, they could navigate at night and sail directly to the Indies in less time than anyone else. This little piece of information made them a lot of money. I heard a story a long time ago about a man who could take a dent out of a motorbike fuel tank. He made a fortune because he was the only man who could do it. One day somebody hid on the roof of his workshop and watched through a hole. He saw dented tanks filled with dried peas which were then wetted. When they expanded they took out the dent. Now anyone can do it.

At the turn of the century anglers had to go to a tackle shop to get a blood knot tied. The tackle shop would tie as many as you paid them for, but wouldn't show you how. It took a determined man called Jock Purvis with a razor blade and a magnifying glass to cut tiny sections and discover its secret. Now it's public domain. The point is that knowledge is there to be used. Once it has become the property of everyone it can no longer be used as an instrument of personal power.

Research into biology and genetics is linked inextricably with the need to exploit the knowledge gained. It becomes vital to protect the investment in research with patents and lawyers. This is the kind of knowledge with actual applications; a hardier strain of wheat, or a spliced gene. It differs from conceptual knowledge which has no application. Philosophical knowledge is knowledge for its own sake. It brings no tangible benefit to those who find it, and sometimes persecution to those who seek it. If there is a pay-off it's hard to quantify; perhaps it's no more than the peace that comes from a centred sense of being.

Agaricus campestris. The Field Mushroom.
Medium sized. Cap 1-5 inches.
White with pink gills.
In pastures. Late summer to autumn.
Edible and boring. Grown commercially worldwide.

nine

It had become obvious to me that the mushroom.man drew his strength from his contact with nature. Yet perhaps it was that very solitary contact that made some of his ideas so distinctly odd. I found the idea that mushrooms were somehow at the root of so much of our culture to be unbelievable and almost certainly drug-induced. To suggest that somehow the world would be a better place if everyone was high on mushrooms was certifiable, to put it mildly. Yet his view of our society split unhappily between a technological world with monotheistic roots and a covert remnant of shamanism was almost believable. Every day I was in contact with bright young minds who longed for magic in their secular lives. This longing expressed itself in endless quests into the New Age. How new this age was in its thinking was something that they never probed. To me it appeared as a re-statement of the Platonic ideals — there was nothing new in it at all.

The mushroom.man seemed to me to have combined elements of his life that I would previously have considered too diverse to combine. Where I grew up rural values and high technology did not sit together. The impression that I was building up of the mushroom.man was of someone who lived an entirely rural existence — by his own description one governed by seventeenth-century technology — and yet who combined that with a high level of competence in new technology, at least as a user. He appeared to draw no distinctions between what I had always assumed to be separate disciplines. Like Greeks in the golden age of Athens, his 'technos' made no distinction between a statue by Praxiteles or a ploughshare made by a blacksmith.

What I needed now was some background information on how he ordered his daily life. How did he fill the average day? How did he cope with the everyday need of obtaining the basics, like shelter, food and heat? Did his computer suffer from the damp? What kind of social interaction did he have?

One thing I had learned from my reading was that there seemed to be a connection between the effects of psychedelic drugs and schizophrenia. There is not only a psychic similarity, but a neurochemical one as well. Osmond and Smythie had suggested in a paper that schizophrenia was caused by an inability of the body to handle its own adrenaline – a substance close in structure to mescaline. In their view a schizophrenic is being poisoned by one of his own body's hallucinogens. This research has been confirmed by Friedhoff and Van Winkle, who were able to isolate another mescaline-like chemical from the urine of schizophrenics. The thought had occurred to me that if this research was correct, then it was equally possible that the effect might be two-way; that is, that prolonged exposure to hallucinogens could bring about the onset of schizophrenia.

If I could find evidence in the mushroom.man's writing of schizophrenia then I had the basis of a good paper which would certainly be noticed. There seemed to be little wrong with my theory that if schizophrenics could produce psychedelic substances in their bodies, then maybe psychedelics could produce schizophrenia. It had a neat circularity to it. I decided to look for instances that would confirm the theory.

I knew by now that whoever this man was at the other end of my modem, he was more comfortable summarizing what he believed were universal truths than describing personal feelings. And yet I felt that perhaps he had actually come to enjoy the process of writing down parts of his experience and sharing it with me. Maybe not, but I hoped that it was true. I asked him to tell me a bit of how he spent his days now, because I was still unclear as to the chronology of what he'd sent me. Two e-mails came within a week of each other. I seemed to have tapped into a vein.

Attn. mushroom.seeker.
Subject: personal history.
27 August.

It was autumn. A weak sun shone through the light cloud cover, a dull, diffused source of light in a grey sky. The fine rain had stopped and the cobwebs on the gorse bushes were highlighted in mist droplets. I stepped out into the moist air, my gun in hand. Sirius, my dog, was hopping about, half-sitting, half-standing, waggling uncontrollably, unable to contain his excitement. Dogs, I think, enjoy the hunt more than humans.

He's a scruffy dog – part sheepdog, part cocker – but a good gun dog. He can retrieve from water or land, and can flush pheasant and rabbits from the densest cover. Maybe twice a week we go through this ritual, Sirius and I. It's an atavistic trade: we both want meat so we co-operate in the hunt. He's an unforgiving partner, quick to sulk if I miss a bird he's spent a long time rooting out. He stares at me and sits down in protest. He needs to be cajoled into starting again.

We worked the edges of the upper wood; the one above the river. There are rabbit burrows all along the forest edge in the sandy banks. Between the burrows and the river is a sward of grass where the rabbits graze. Our technique is to approach from the woods so that to get to the burrows they have to run towards the gun. Mostly they scatter instead and Sirius puts them out of their scrapes and hides so that they bolt over the open ground where I can shoot them. I rarely take more than two on any day, one for me, one for the dog. We moved slowly through the wood, toward the rabbit burrows, Sirius never more than ten yards from me, checking under every fallen tree, in every stand of brown and brittle bracken. A few deer droppings, some tracks in the soft earth of the path. Mushroomy, damp smells rise from the leaf litter. Slower now, as we come to the river, senses heightened, walking carefully through the dry and broken twigs. As we reached the bank Sirius dashed forward into the grazing rabbits.

I shot a big buck, two or three years old, torn ears and a heavy scruff on his neck. I waited for Sirius to bring it to me, but he didn't; he was nosing around a gorse clump. As I walked toward the rabbit, a hind leg still twitching, the whirr of wings made me turn. A cock pheasant took off, heading downstream. I wasn't really ready, my gun was down, my concentration gone. I should have kept my eye on the gorse clump just in case. By the time I had the gun to my shoulder the bird was flying fast and far – a long shot. I fired and it came down in the river wounded and flapping. Sirius brought it back, wet and still alive. I pulled its neck and hung it on the strings of my belt, followed by the rabbit. A good day.

We walked back towards the house, the catch banging off my leg as we walked. Approaching the bridge I saw a lone figure leaning on the railings. As we got closer a young woman turned and stared. I'm never quite sure how to greet strangers out here; I've noticed that city people like you to ignore them, they seem uncomfortable with a greeting. Even on the top of mountains I've had them pretend not to see me. It's bizarre; miles from anywhere their strange manners dictate that you can observe all of nature with the exception of people. They still behave as they do in a crowded street. This woman's gaze didn't falter; she kept her eyes on me, the rabbit, the pheasant and the dog. Every time I looked back toward her I met her eyes. I suppose I could have crossed to the other side of the bridge but that seemed an odd way to behave. As we came alongside her she spoke.

'You've got blood on your hands.'

I looked down at my hands, not blooded but a little feathered. I couldn't think of anything to say, but I felt that a comment this bald deserved a reply.

'Not really.'

'Of course you do. And you've got blood on your shoes.'

The rabbit was dripping blood from its mouth, spatters were on my shoes and a little on my trousers.

'It's disgusting,' she continued.

'Look, I don't kill for fun, I kill for food.'

'People like you should be shot.'

'People like you should mind their own business.'

I walked on, angry that I could think of nothing better to say. Angry that this woman should have made me angry. I'd been enjoying the day, the walk, the successful hunt. Even the bloody dog was happy. Who the hell do these people think they are? I have the right to eat what I please, and kill it too if that's the way to obtain it. Fuck it, it's no one's business but mine what I do. Jesus, these interfering, woolly-minded, lentil-eating freaks should stay near their local health food shop or whole-food or whatever the fuck they call it. Proselytes. Can't leave well enough alone, no, they have to go around forcing their half-arsed opinions on the rest of us. I came here to get away from this sort of shit. I'll turn the skin of this rabbit into a hat and wear it, just to annoy this silly woman.

My thoughts stilled for long enough to hear footsteps behind me. I turned: she was following me. I stopped, hoping she would walk past and out of my life. She stopped beside me and patted the dog. The stupid dog rolled over and let her rub his belly; silly beast has no idea of dignity.

'What's his name?'

'Sirius.'

'You smell of dead animals.'

'Me or the dog?'

'You.'

I looked over her head to the forest. I counted slowly to ten. I looked at her and saw that she had a very pretty face; thin and bony but attractive. Large blue eyes. Her hair was light brown, hazel; thick and shiny. I couldn't make out much else; she wore a padded coat and cords tucked into wellies. I wondered did she have thick ankles.

'Do you live near?' she asked.

'Just across that field.' I wanted to say it was none of her business, but it didn't come out.

'I'm thinking of moving here.'

'Don't.'

'Why not?'

'If you find death so offensive you'll never hack it here. Death's all around, darling.'

'Don't patronize me.'

'I'm not. I'm serious.'

'I thought that was your dog's name.' She laughed at her little joke, a tinkling laugh that brought an unwilling smile to my lips. I wanted not to like her, her insulting tongue, her odd beliefs. She looked really good when she laughed, soft, female and sexy. I really hate that in myself, a whiff of pheromone and I'm fighting to remain a man rather than a lump of putty. I hate the weakness of it; the beguiling allure that makes me think of beds and warm bodies instead of responding to her insults. It demeans me; if this was a man there'd be no bother, I'd tell him to fuck off and if that didn't work I could punch him. Instead I find myself trying to make myself attractive in the hope of getting laid. What a pathetic way to order your life.

'Don't be angry.' She tilted her head to one side and her hair moved like shiny gold threads on her collar.

'I'm not angry. Just surprised at your directness.'

'I'm always direct.'

'Where were you thinking of moving to?'

She pointed downstream. 'The old mill, there.'

'It's a ruin.'

'I'll do it up.' She looked upstream across the field to my house. 'We'll be neighbours.'

I wasn't sure what to make of this. I mean, directness is something I find hard to take in a stranger – but in a neighbour? I'd meet her a lot if she lived in the old mill. It could be awful. And yet she was pretty. Attractive. I liked her laugh. But then again, she had little in common with me. Anyway, who says she'd find me attractive? Maybe she's already got a man. Or a woman. Who knows. Stupid thoughts; wondering about her and me. I might never see her again.

'I didn't know the mill was for sale.'

'It's not. It's got about twenty owners, most of them live abroad. Half of them don't even know they've been left it. No forwarding addresses. I'm just going to move in.'

'What if they find out?'

'What if they don't?' She laughed again and I liked it. It was a good sound.

I started to mumble a goodbye and move on.

'Do you mind if I walk with you?'

'If you like.'

We walked, Sirius running forward, back to us and forward again. She moved from the side where the game hung to the other side. We were silent, she for whatever reason, I because I couldn't think of anything to say. I was determined to say nothing banal.

'Why do you want to live around here?' just slipped out.

'I'm following my ley line.'

'Your ley line.'

'I marked on a map where I was born, then where I grew up, then where I live now. It makes a straight line. Isn't that weird?'

'Suppose so.' That three random points should make a straight line isn't that odd. I mean, I'm not going to calculate the odds, but it can't be too unlikely.

'So I drew the line on the map and projected it. It comes through here.'

Here and a million other places along the way, I thought. Why do people only ever pick out the bits that they want and ignore the rest?

'What about the other direction?'

'That's north. My heart is pulled to the south. It had to be this way.'

'I see.'

I didn't, of course. This is a kind of logic that I am unfamiliar with. Maybe this is what they mean when they say that it's a gender thing. The whole process of this reasoning seemed unlike anything else. Why should points on a map make any difference one way or another? It's a kind of divination, I suppose, like yarrow sticks or tarot; random event generators from which we hope to make sense.

'I couldn't find the circle,' she announced.

'The what?'

'The stone circle – I couldn't find it.'

'What stone circle?'

'I think it should be there.' She pointed to the field in front of my house. 'I've got an old map that shows one. I might be wrong, but I think it's marked in that field. It's another reason that I wanted to follow my ley. It's a power spot.'

It flashed before me. Greg sitting on a stone in the middle of the henge. In front of my house.

'What year is this map?'

'1776.'

'Can I see it?'

'Sure. It's in the car.'

Where the forest track meets the main road there's a clearing where you can park a car. We were walking that way and I felt a sense of excitement. If she was right then my dream or vision had some grounds of reality in it. I mean, if the henge was on the map, placed where I'd seen it, then I had to reassess. I'd never thought of moving through time any way but forward. Or maybe I'd stayed here and the henge had moved forward two hundred years. Either way I wanted to see the map.

She drove an old, small green van. Of course, I thought, green in everything but its emissions. I could see that the inside was a tip. Wouldn't surprise me if it had mice. Paper, litter, bags, boxes, clothes, all strewn around front and back.

'I know it's in here somewhere.'

As she rummaged, bent over through the door, I tried to imagine what was under the bulk of the winter clothing. Thin face and hands, probably a flat, wide bum. Thin thighs? Maybe a gap at the top, a crotch gap. Liked that. She was still rooting. Maybe this was a waste of time. Maybe she'd imagined the map. Imagined the stone circle. I couldn't make out anything of her legs. Pity it wasn't summer.

'Here it is.'

'Great. Can I see?'

She handed me a book, *Dolmens, Henges and Triliths*.

'Page 87, I think.'

She was right. There was a fold-out map of the area to a good scale. A house was marked where mine stands, a stone circle in the field in front. I turned to the title-page and found the date. Published by Eben Pringle & Sons, MDC-CLXXVI.

'Found it?'

'Yeah. Do you mind if we walk down again with the book and check it out?'

'No, I'd be interested. Let's go.'

The book covered most of this part of the country, listing the standing stones, the ring forts, the henges and dolmens. I flicked through as we walked. This whole area was a mass of megalithic works, hundreds of them.

'Do you know much about stone circles?' she asked.

'Not much. They marked the periods of the moon, didn't they?'

'And the sun. Mid-winter was the important one. It marked the new year, and therefore you knew when to plant your corn. Guessing gave bad results as a rule.'

'I see.'

We crossed the stile into the field, Sirius forcing himself through the sheep wire. I orientated myself with the map.

The field seemed to be exactly as it was two hundred years ago, the boundary hedges unchanged.

'It should be here.' I stood where the middle should be. For a brief moment I had two images before me; the one I normally see and the one I'd seen once. Like a dissolve on film, for an instant the stones were nearly there, transparent, but there.

'You see them, don't you?'

'What?'

'The stones. You see them.'

'I did, just for a second. They're gone.'

'I wonder where they put them.'

'Who?'

'The people who took them away. A lot of circles were dismantled by fundamentalist Christians who thought that they were pagan temples. They thought they were tied in with witchcraft and black magic.'

'They couldn't have taken them far. They're big stones.'

I began to walk the ditches around the field. Hawthorn, blackthorn, bramble, bracken and gorse. A dry-stone wall in decay, fallen and overgrown, like a skeleton inside the browning autumnal vegetation. She walked some ten paces in front of me, copying me. I get irritated at things like that, mainly because I don't like the feeling of pettiness it inspires in me. But if there's a discovery to be made, I should make it. It's my field and my idea.

'Look,' she said, 'look at that in the wall.'

I walked up to her and looked into the ditch. At the bottom of it a large granite boulder lay on its side, forming the base of the wall. It had to be from the circle.

'There's another one.' She pointed a few yards further on.

I hate having my ideas pre-empted. Now she gets the credit for the discovery, even though checking the ditches was my idea. I turned to her and said: 'I had a feeling we might find them in the wall. They couldn't have moved stones that big very far.'

We moved vaguely toward the middle of the field. I was uneasy about the circle and my previous vision of it. This woman made me feel uncomfortable as well. How did she know that I'd seen the stones, however briefly, just now? A guess? Also I'd just spent a half hour or so in her company, despite feeling annoyed at her rudeness. Just because she was a bit attractive I was wasting time with her, sharing personal visions unwillingly. She was invading me, that was it, invading a private part of me. Invading private parts. I would, if she'd let me. God, how I hate this stuff. Like a mental, internalized version of Tourette's syndrome. Smutty mind in a ravaged body. *Mens insana in corpore insano.*

There'd been no woman in my life for four months or so, and I missed that. A German hitch-hiker had taken up residence with me for a couple of months in the spring and early summer. One morning I found her packed. She thanked me for letting her stay, gave me a kiss and said it was time that she went home. Said she'd be in touch, but I never heard from her again. Like a re-run of Jane's goodbye. Maybe I'm not what women want for a long-term partnership. A summer with my right hand and fantasies for company.

'Can I see your house?'

'What? Yes, yes of course. I'll make you a cup of tea.'

A cup of tea? What a dumb offer. What should I have offered? A drink? Warm up in front of the fire. That's it. Get her warm; she'll take off that lumpy coat. See what she looks like. We walked up the path to the house.

'Move the cat and make yourself comfortable. I'll just stoke up the fire.' I put on some dry logs and pumped the bellows rhythmically. A flame. She had the cat on her lap, stroking it. I went into the kitchen to put on the kettle.

'Milk and sugar?'

'Neither, thanks.'

Figures. Plain tea. I took mine with no milk for once, but I put in sugar. I gave her a mug and took off my coat, hanging it behind the front door. I sat down opposite her, Sirius lying by her feet. I dismantled my gun and started to clean it.

'Can't you do that later? I hate guns.'

'Sorry.'

I put the gun on the wall. Why am I saying sorry for doing something in my own home? Some people's sensibilities are bloody demanding. I remember most of Jane's friends were vegetarian. When they came to us for a meal I had to eat brown rice. When we went to their house I had to eat brown rice. I always wanted to say 'I gave you your rice and lentils, where's my bloody steak?' I sat down again. She was intent on the cat. She had taken off her boots and was sitting with her legs stretched out. Her ankles didn't look thick through her long socks.

'So when are you thinking of moving down here?'

'Today. I've moved.'

'But the mill's a ruin. Where are you going to stay?'

'I brought my tent. I'll set it up down by the river and get a roof onto the mill. With a bit of help.' She looked up and smiled at me. Oh, now I see. I'm supposed to do the work in exchange for a winning smile. What am I? A white knight?

'Are you sure that's a good idea? We're coming into winter. It gets cold, wet. It snows. A tent won't help much.'

'If it gets bad maybe you'll offer me shelter.'

'I suppose. But it's not much of a plan. I mean you don't know me. I don't know you.'

'I know quite a lot about you.'

'How? Telepathically?'

'No. From Dave.'

'Dave?'

'Dutch Dave.'

'You know him?'

'I was married to him, I'm Clair. He's told me quite a lot about you. I was curious when I found out my ley went right through your house.'

'Ah.'

That was the best I could manage. I nodded, trying not to look stupid. She's known who I am since we were standing on the bridge. I wondered if I'd ever told Dave about my vision of the stones. Maybe she knows about that, too. I didn't know Dave was married, or had ever been married; he'd never mentioned a wife or a Clair. She stood up.

'Mind if use your loo?'

'No, of course. Straight through.'

'Thanks.'

This wasn't an invasion of privacy, this was a full-scale premeditated D-day assault. She wants to stay here while she may or not do up the mill. Probably wants me to do all the work anyway. Suppose I had crossed to the other side of the bridge, not looked at her, perhaps I wouldn't feel so entangled. Stupid dog let her stroke his belly, got me into a conversation. She came back into the room.

'Nice, your house. Not much on housework are you?'

Is that what's on offer? Do the housework? Judging by the state of her car it wasn't much of a bargaining position.

'It's not the most important thing to me.'

'Obviously not.'

I went to the mantelpiece and took my tobacco.

'You want a roll-up?'

'No thanks. I'd prefer if you didn't. I don't want to inhale your smoke.'

There's an obvious reply here that I should have, but didn't, use. Step outside then, while I smoke in my house.

'OK.' I put the tobacco back.

'It's bad for you, you know.'

You'd have to have lived on another planet for the past twenty years not to know that. It's my choice; bad maybe, but mine. Like killing rabbits or taking sugar in my tea. My choice. She stood up and took off her coat, throwing it over the back of the sofa. A bulky sweater made just as good a job of hiding her shape as the coat had done. It was beginning to get dark outside. I turned on a light.

'Turn it off. The fire-light's lovely.'

I did as I was told, but I could feel rebellion growing in my belly. I looked at her in the growing dimness, flickering light playing over her. She looked up.

'Sorry, I'm being demanding. I'm used to getting my own way.'

'So I see.'

'Turn on the light if you want to.'

'No. You're right. This light is fine. You want another mug?'

'Please.'

I was being weak. She was manipulating me shamelessly. Instead of offering to walk her back to her car before the light went, I was offering her another mug of tea. Another half hour of hospitality by which time it would be dark. I began to realize that instead of me luring her into my house for some vague, undefined hope of sex, it was she who had set the stage and choreographed every step. Whatever deal I made now was the one I was going to live with. Full testicles were leading my reasoning one way; good sense pointed in an entirely different direction. I brought her in another mug of tea and sat down, warming myself at the fire. It was a good blaze, and I threw on a few more logs.

'It's getting dark.'

'Yes. Would you mind if I stayed here tonight?'

This is it. It's out; spoken. Can't be recalled. Make a deal, and make it good.

'Sure. I've only got one bed, though.'

'I've got a sleeping bag in the car.'

'It's a long walk in the dark.'

She smiled. I could see the corners of her mouth twitch in the soft light.

'You're right. I'll get it in the morning. I'm hungry. What have you got to eat?'

'Pheasant or rabbit.'

'I don't eat dead animals.'

'I don't eat living ones.'

'Got any rice or potatoes? Beans?'

'Potatoes I think. Sirius and me will eat the rabbit.'

'Do you have to?'

'Yes I do. I'm hungry; so's he.'

She got up and went to the kitchen. I watched the flames. So it was agreed. She'd live here, with the fiction that she'd be going to do up the mill. I wouldn't smoke in the house, she'd help with the house-keeping and sleep in my bed. I would continue to eat meat, but she wouldn't cook it. Would it work? Only time would tell; anyway I was reasoning no further than tonight. An end to four months of celibacy. The future could look after itself.

We worked in the kitchen together, in silence except for the odd request as to where things were kept. I casseroled the rabbit, she made a vegetable stew. We ate at the kitchen table, unspoken questions hovering in the air between us.

'Dave says you were married.'

'Actually Jane and I never got married. We lived together for eight years.'

'Why did you leave her?'

'I didn't. She left me.'

'Oh. Why?'

'I don't know. She married now; she's got two kids.'

'I see.'

After we ate we sat by the fire and listened to music. I went out for wood and sat on the wood-pile, watching the odd star through breaks in the clouds and smoked a roll-up. I could see Clair's shadow through the window moving around on the wall. I wondered what she was doing. When I went in she had the cushions from the sofa laid out, like a bed, in front of the fire.

'I could sleep here, if you prefer.'

'No, you'll get cold when the fire goes down. Sleep in my bed.'

She put the cushions back while I placed the fire-guard. I thought we'd decided the sleeping arrangements. We went into the bedroom and a little self-consciously started to undress. I got into bed first and watched her. She removed everything except a tee-shirt and got in beside me.

'It's lovely and warm,' she said, pulling the covers up tight to her chin.

'Electric blanket.' I said.

I lay, supported by an elbow, looking at her. Her eyes met mine.

'Do you want to have sex with me?' she asked.

'Yes.'

'Look, you can use my body for sex, but I won't be contributing. I mean, don't expect anything from me. And no kissing. OK?'

I'd have agreed to anything. It wasn't what I wanted, but it was better than nothing. Women have to be clever about sex. They have to know exactly how to ration it. Give a man too much, too readily, and he loses respect. Give him too little and he'll look elsewhere. It's all in the dosage. I don't think they teach it in schools, but I've never met a woman who doesn't understand it perfectly.

'Take off your tee-shirt.'

She sat up, and like women always do, took her arms out of the sleeves before she pulled it over her head. She lay back and I looked. Wide shoulders, long neck, small breasts with prominent nipples, a small mole between them, flat stomach with a slightly protruding belly button. I pulled the covers down. Big bush of pubic hair, even on the tops of her thighs. Long thighs, soft skinned. I stroked them. She lay immobile, letting me explore her body, but without reaction. I stroked her nipples and bent over to kiss them, she pushed me away gently. No kissing.

'Get on top of me.' I said, hoping that she would.

She sat astride me and I tried to have sex with her, but I couldn't. She was dry and tight and the harder I pushed the

more it hurt me. The pain eventually made me lose my erection. I said nothing, and she simply got off and lay down with
her back to me.

    'Goodnight.'

    'Goodnight.'

    I turned off the light and slept.

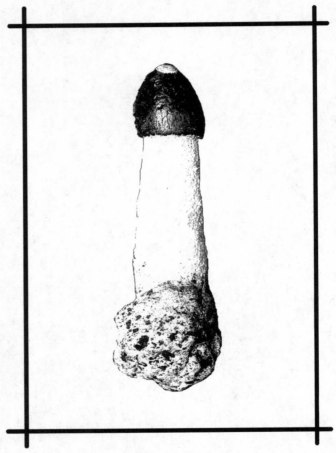

Phallus impudicus. The Stinkhorn.
4-10 inches high. White with black slimy head.
Disgusting-smelling when mature. Attracts flies from miles away.
Grows on rotting wood. Summer to late autumn.
Edible when immature, but not tasty.
Said to be aphrodisiac, probably because of its shape.

ten

The second e-mail of the same week continued the story of Clair's arrival in his life. I was in no position to judge the mushroom.man's odd relationship with her, since my own personal life was virtually without human contact. But the mushroom.man that had the relationship he was describing seemed oddly at variance with how I had imagined him to be. To be blunt, anyone who hoped to control an internal universe really ought to be able to modify the excesses of someone else's behaviour – especially if you're sharing a house with her. This was, however, precisely the sort of topic that I never discussed when e-mailing him: I felt that if I became too intrusive he might simply cease to communicate.

None the less what he had sent me was a profoundly personal description of a relationship that seemed to be recent. If it was recent, then the mushroom.man was still able to manage his life with some degree of competence – although by any standards it was eccentric. What was becoming clearer to me now was the link between his mushroom world and the world of his everyday life.

I was still looking for evidence of schizophrenia in his writings; specifically anxiety, emotional instability and inappropriateness of feelings. The classical definition of schizophrenia – believing that the self and the world are unreal – was obviously one that fitted the mushroom.man like a glove. It was already plain to me that he regarded reality as something that was essentially fluid rather than fixed. This in itself was insufficient for a diagnosis of schizophrenia, but it was certainly a pointer.

It was at this stage that I finally decided I would write a paper to support my thesis that prolonged use of psychedelics could cause schizophrenia. I began to collate my ideas and drew, wherever I could, on some of the mushroom.man's more bizarre writings as exemplars of poor reality contact among chronic abusers. His relationship with Clair seemed to me to be a good example of his inability to deal with reality.

Detachment and dissociation are common in habitual users of illicit drugs. It's possible that the drugs are not the cause, but that rather it is the personality types that seek out the drugs that are already inclined to disorganization and have poor connections with society at large. Either way this self-destructiveness can be found frequently among users. A typical, textbook profile of hallucinogen users would be artistic and intelligent people who have limited contact with ordinary society. In a sense this is a pointer toward a predisposition to schizophrenia, the limited contact making connection with ordinary reality vague and amorphous.

I mentioned this to one of my students, who pointed out that the dissociation of which I was speaking was similar in many respects to certain forms of ecstatic religious experience. That Teresa of Avila, John of the Cross or Joseph of Cupertino inhabited a reality that differed from that of their peers cannot be in doubt. Yet to a Christian their ecstasies are examples not of lack of reality contact, but rather of communion with the sublime.

The mystical notion of detaching the body from the world has also been a part of the Christian tradition. Christ himself exhorted his disciples: 'Take therefore no thought for tomorrow: for the morrow shall take thought for the things of itself.' It's a piece of advice that seems as apt for a junkie as is it for a disciple. The next e-mail confirmed much of this for me.

Attn. mushroom.seeker.
Subject: more history.
5 September.

I was in the kitchen sterilizing Petri plates in the pressure cooker. Clair walked in and watched me.

'What are you doing?'
'Sterilizing plates.'

'Why?'

'I culture spores on them. They have to be sterile or I get contamination from the airborne spores in the house.'

'Why bother?'

She walked out the room and put Joni Mitchell on loudly in the sitting room. I shut the door, but could still hear the music. I've been through this ritual of cleansing plates hundreds of times; it's a purification ceremony that I've always done in silence. It's not important, not part of the ritual, it's just that I'm used to doing things in that way.

I took out the Petri plates and transferred them to my sterile box. I began the sterilization of the Mason jars filled with rye medium. Clair pushed open the door and stood in the doorway.

'Can't you stop doing that? You're steaming up all the windows. I can't see out.'

'I'll be finished soon.'

'Jesus, I wish you would.'

She walked out again, leaving the door open. I pushed it shut hard and went back to the range. Growing cultures on agar is time-consuming. It demands concentration. If you hurry it and make mistakes, then your punishment is contamination and hence wasted time, medium, and spores. Doing it well pleases me, I really enjoy the satisfaction of a job well done. Besides, the result of the work is the fruit of my labour and the fruit of knowledge. Years ago Greg had sent some photostatted pages of instructions on growing psilocybin mushrooms. Although they grow abundantly in the wild they don't grow all year round. The process of growing mycelium on agar and then inoculating a rye medium means that fresh specimens are available to me all year round. I get pure, clean mushrooms, untouched by slugs, maggots and flies. I know the strength of the culture that I use. I like to stay close to ten milligrams of psilocybin; that's a couple of ounces of my home-grown fresh ones. Clair opened the door again.

'Are you finished yet?'

'Nearly.'

'Jesus Christ.'

A draught came in, blowing dust about. She shut the door and then I heard the front door slam. She was not easy to live with. Like Jane she had no time for my mushrooms. No interest in the worlds to which they led.

She'd been staying for about six months and life wasn't easy. She was increasingly demanding and increasingly ungenerous. A couple of weeks before, she'd moved out of my bed and onto the sofa. Sex between us had reminded me of having sex with a hooker – except Clair didn't even attempt to fake an orgasm. It made me feel sordid for using her body; in a way I was grateful she wasn't beside me any more at night for my hormones to overcome my sense. But I was angry.

Angry because I felt used. Because my house was no longer my own. I hate to admit it, but angry as well because she was expensive to have around. Not in big things; just in the total of hundreds of small things. She used lots of hot water, the hair-dryer every day, huge amounts of toilet paper that blocked the drains, burnt logs all night since she'd begun sleeping on the sofa, never shut doors or turned off lights – just used resources incessantly. I mean the log pile didn't get there by accident. It was three full days' work of chopping and stacking; enough, I thought, to see the winter through. Now I was starting to think maybe not. I just kept thinking there has to be a trade if we're living together. It has to have something in it for both if it's to work. I could see what she was getting out of it: a roof, food and warmth. But me? A whole lot of irritation, that's what. I don't think I was asking for a lot. Companionship on long winter nights, some-one to share things with. She was sharing all right – every-thing I had – but there was bugger-all companionship. Lots of niggles, arguments, discontent. I had no idea how to put an end to it; I immersed myself instead in my dreams and in my mushrooms.

A lot of things were beginning to gel in my mind, despite the distractions that Clair caused. Disparate ideas began to coalesce, making new connections. I was increasingly drawn to earth magic, shamanism, the old beliefs about Gaia. Monotheistic cosmologies seemed too male-oriented, run by men for men to the exclusion of women. The earth cults all seemed more female, less analytical, more mystical. And yet the female seemed to be the part of my life that didn't fuse in any way. All my relationships had been unsatisfactory in one way or another. There wasn't one I could point to and say 'that one at least was complete', not even for a day. All flawed.

I prepared the Petri plates and put them into the sterile box. I tidied the kitchen, putting things where Clair liked them to be. I took down a Mason jar from a shelf, picked and weighed out 50 grams of fresh mushrooms. The day was windy but not cold, clouds hurried low over the forest; there was an odd burst of sunlight. I ate the mushrooms, put on a coat and made my way out.

When I was a little boy I had had a recurring dream: I visited an empty house – always the same house. I got to know it well, all the rooms, even the garden. It was not a house that I knew in my waking state, it only came to life in my dreams. Even today I could draw it, make a plan of the interior. I went there so often it became real. Nothing of any import ever happened there; I just visited it and explored it. The same thing had begun to happen with the mushrooms. I kept finding the stone circle. The difference was that this time I felt that there was something to discover. I was sure that there was a reason that the stones appeared to me.

Outside the house the wind was strong. I walked, head bowed, toward the forest, immersed in my thoughts. I sat on a fallen tree at the forest's edge watching the sky. A jay chattered somewhere in the woods, but apart from that it was quiet. As I waited for the psilocybin to take effect I tried to define where my life was leading me. I had that feeling that there was a purpose to it, all I had to do was discover it. It's the same feeling that prompts people to embrace religion: the need to feel that there is a point to it all. I had been content for years with the idea that the answer was simply to be a part of it, like a worker bee in a hive. The individual life is of no consequence, it's the survival of the hive, the particular genetic package, that matters. Now I was struck with the feeling that my life had a purpose; that all the events that had led me to this very spot were destined. A strange feeling, since I had no idea of what that purpose might be.

An urge to see if the stones were visible got me up and walking. Crossing the river once more I saw the shimmering outlines of the henge. There were people, or what appeared to be people in a circle, doing some kind of dance. I approached slowly, with a little trepidation. The only time I'd ever seen people in the circle was when I'd seen Greg sitting in the middle. It was a bizarre sight. A satyr, Pan-like, was holding hands with two women; a circle of three slowly turning to the sound of some unheard music. As I walked up to them they stopped and turned to me. The satyr's face was Greg's, the women were White Cloud and Yelena. They looked serious, as though concentrating. It was Yelena who spoke.

'We knew you'd come.'

I said nothing; I could feel waves beginning in my belly which pulsed through my body and into my brain making the sight before me quiver, like a badly tracked video. I was disturbed to find these two women in my vision – I had rejected them on our only previous meeting as shallow and silly. Now they were here to confront me, I was sure of that. My eyes were drawn to the satyr. He stood about my height, thick hair from the waist down covering his legs but not his enormous penis, which hung, fat and long, above the russet hair. His face was definitely Greg's, but I couldn't relate to him as Greg.

I found it hard to make sense of this. Why were these two

odd women here with my friend assuming the form of a satyr? The picture before me began to pulse, each beat of my heart made it throb. It was as though the two realities – that of the empty field and that of the stones – were almost in harmony but not quite in phase. Perhaps it was my unwillingness to confront these women that made the vision unstable. I found myself focusing unwillingly on the satyr's penis, fascinated by its size. As I watched, it too began to throb, growing larger with each beat, until I was staring at a monstrous erection.

The satyr lay on his back, and as though in a well-rehearsed play, the women moved quickly to him. Yelena lifted her skirt and squatted carefully over the massive erection, lowering herself slowly onto it. Almost in time with her White Cloud lifted her skirt and began to squat over the satyr's face. His tongue protruded obscenely as she sat. I could feel the blood in my temples, I could hear its rush. I watched the bestial thighs rise and fall, heard the women moan. I must have closed my eyes – when I opened them a second later I saw Greg, Yelena and White Cloud sitting in a circle. No satyr, no pornographic tableau.

'Come and sit down,' said Greg. 'You've got a wild imagination, you know.'

'What do you mean?'

'Repressed sexuality,' offered Yelena.

'Filthy mind,' said White Cloud.

They began to laugh in a childish, giggling way. I felt myself start to relax, the throbbing was ebbing away. I walked to the nearest stone and touched it. It was cold, a little damp, and very solid. I came back to Greg and sat down. He smiled at me and said:

'Maybe deep down you've always seen me as a sexual goat.'

I had trouble with this. This was my vision, I thought. The stones, these three, are here because I'm imagining them. I created this reality with mushrooms – and yet here were the creatures of my imagination acting out some buried fantasies of mine, and offering to discuss them – as though they were sentient beings. I'd made sense of my last encounter with Greg at these stones by reasoning him as a ghost. That fitted what I'd seen, and needed no further analysis. A ghost, a spirit, a shade. Whatever. This time he was reading thoughts of mine that even I was only dimly aware of. I knew the stones were not part of everyday reality, I knew Greg was dead and so not part of everyday reality, but these women lived not far from me – in everyday reality. How could such different elements combine here, before my eyes?

'He's obviously not getting it enough,' Yelena said, smiling at White Cloud and rubbing her hand between her legs. She seemed aware of how uncomfortable it made me, and relished it. I looked at Greg.

'It's OK, they're only doing it to annoy,' he said. 'You don't have to look if you don't want to.'

'Do you know them?' I asked.

'Of course. I met them in the States.'

'I met them here.'

'God you can be stupid. Of course you did, I sent them here. You surely don't think your life is an accident, do you?'

White Cloud put her hand on Greg's knee. 'After he died it was me who phoned you. Greg spoke of you and Jane a lot, didn't you Greg?'

'I did. I told them about these hills, the magic of the earth, its history of druids and shamans. It's a special place, a place of wonder and mystery.'

Yelena sat upon her haunches. 'It's a place full of jerks.'

'Greg, do you know Dave?' I asked.

'Dave who?'

'Dutch Dave.'

'No, never met him.'

'Or Clair?'

'No, don't know her either.'

I felt relieved. A piece of my life, a thread, that didn't connect to Greg. Something that I could call my own; something that didn't fit into these bizarre visions.

'This is no vision.' Greg grabbed my hand hard. 'I can pinch you.'

'I know Dave well,' said White Cloud, 'he's my lover. We trade, you know. He gives me coke and I give him sex.'

'While we're on the subject of sex again, I'll tell you something else I know.' Yelena stared at me.

'What's that?'

'You had a wank thinking about me.'

'What?'

'You did, didn't you?'

'How do you know that? Maybe you imagined it.'

'No. You do all the imagining. Do you want me to tell them what you imagined between us?'

'No. Please don't.'

It was true. My thoughts and fantasies seemed to be common currency in this world. It was true, I had thought of her – but I don't expect, or look for, sense or reason in fantasies. I've fantasized over huge, obese women, but I don't think it translates into the world outside of fantasy. I didn't find Yelena attractive; it was an aberration of the moment. Once again I was irritated that a woman had some power over me.

Is that what celibacy is about? Sex and secrecy. If you have a secret and want to keep it, then you offer a weapon to anyone who finds it. I've always tried to keep my life an open book for this very reason. If everything you do is known, then you can never be blackmailed on any level. Openness is power; secrets are time-bombs waiting to explode into your life.

'OK, Yelena,' I said, 'tell them.'

She looked at me carefully, the same look that I'd seen her give White Cloud over the dinner table.

'You really want me to?'

'Yeah, sure. Go for it.'

'No. Maybe not.'

Perhaps I imagined it, but I thought I saw a blush, or the beginnings of one. I felt elated – the shame was no longer mine. Certainly it wasn't hers, but it didn't feel part of me any more either. Funny how so small a thing can be a liberation.

'That's good,' Greg said to me, 'never be afraid of truth.'

White Cloud stood up and held out a hand to Yelena. They stood together for a moment, and then kissed for what seemed like a long time. They walked off, hand in hand.

'I met them at a party.'

'Yeah?'

'I thought they were, that they were, a bit shallow.'

'Yeah?'

'I mean, if they're friends of yours, maybe there's more to them than I thought.'

'There always is.'

'What?'

'More to it than you think.'

Greg got up and stretched. He yawned and I noticed his teeth were no longer black and broken. He pushed his hair back, just as he always did. He saw me looking.

'Happy to see me?'

'You know I am. It's just that I get confused sometimes. I'm not sure on what level we're meeting. You know, whether you're really here or whether I'm imagining it.'

'Comes to the same thing really, doesn't it?'

'Does it?'

'Of course. If I can say things that surprise you or are new to you then it's a fruitful meeting. For both of us.'

I hadn't thought of that before. It hadn't occurred to me that these meetings with Greg may have been curious to him too.

'Remember the last time we met here, in the circle?'

'Yes.'

'Remember we went to the house and Jane was there?'

'What's your point?'

'Well, when I thought about it later I thought that some-how I'd become a part of, or I'd got inside your memory of things. I mean, the house looked like mine, but it wasn't.'

'Is that a question?'

'No, but I want to know this. Was that, is this, your mem-ory – your experience – or is it mine?'

'Some's mine, some's yours. What did you expect?'

'I don't know.'

We sat still, in silence. Imps were running around and between the stones. Like cartoon imps, small and darting.

I see them occasionally when I've eaten mushrooms. I don't know what they are or what they do, but they've never done me any harm. They're just a part of that world and I accept them as that. I wondered whether Greg was aware of his death.

'Greg?'

'Yeah.'

'Do you think about death?'

'No more than you think about life. I just accept it, like you accept living. Think about it, all your questions – the ones that dog your days – are about life. You hardly ever think about death.'

'That's true, I suppose. I can't really think about death; I don't know what to expect.'

'No one does.'

We lapsed into silence again. I was trying to control the effect of the mushrooms, fearful that a lapse of concentration might make Greg disappear. I wanted him there, I needed him to help me through this. So many threads seemed to con-nect directly to him. Whatever was happening to me, he was a part of. It was Greg who broke the silence.

'Who's Clair?'

'She lives with me. Well, not like a lover – she lives in my house.'

'Why?'

'I wish I knew. She just sort of moved in.'

'Just sort of moved in.'

'I know, it's stupid. It seemed like a good idea at the time. Anyway she needs somewhere to stay.'

'How chivalrous of you. You know your problem, don't you?'

'What?'

'You let things happen to you. You're not an actor, you're an observer. Things and people come to you and you just accept it. You never make things happen. Your life's like a silhouette; it's defined not by what you do but by what's been done to you. It's a negative image.'

He was right. I'd only ever drifted into things, never plunged. I realized I wasn't in control. It was stupid, I know, all I wanted was a little simplicity in my life, some harmony and peace. Clair was the antithesis to all that. As I thought of her I realized that I'd have to deal with her when I got home. Her rages, her shouting. Why was I so weak?

'I have to go now.'

'Why, Greg?'

'It's time, old buddy. We'll meet again.'

He walked off slowly, leaving me with my thoughts. What strange path were the mushrooms leading me down? Talking with the dead, watching fantasies materialize. Maybe this is the stuff of insanity. Maybe. This at least had some kind of logic. The real world had none of that. That was a truly insane world. Depends on where you stand, I suppose. I could survive so long as this crazy world remained only in my head; as long as I could still function in the real world.

But that's the problem, I can't keep it a secret, I don't want any time-bombs waiting to explode in my face. I can exorcize this madness, if madness it is, by exposing it, externalizing it. It's not such a crazy way to live. All I'm doing is exploring other worlds – no more than any of us do each night in our dreams.

A movement at the far end of the field caught my eye. As

my eyes focused on it I could see a file of people walking toward the henge. They were intoning a strange high-pitched chant. Five men led the group, dressed in what looked like gowns of thick, green felt. They wore oak leaves woven through their long hair. They approached the central trilith, and each in turn laid his sprigs of oak on the stones. The chant continued, and the five men took up position around the centre. As they sang I began to notice that each of the stones was surrounded by lines. I could see them as clearly as isobars on a map. They swirled and eddied and then appeared to settle. Each stone was surrounded by lines, some ran around the stones in spirals up to the top. Each of the five men appeared to be standing in a whirlpool of lines. Still they chanted, now more rhythmically, and with each beat of the chant the lines around the stones began to throb. The song had been imperceptibly getting faster and as it reached its crescendo the whirlpools of lines at the feet of the men suddenly rose up and enveloped each of them, just as they had the stones. The men quivered as the encircling lines embraced their bodies. Almost as one they shrieked; a high, long, piercing call. The lines disappeared and all five fell down, as though the swirling lines had been their means of support. The spectators ran up to them and bathed their faces with water. One by one they stood up and then joined hands. They remained in silence for what seemed an eternity, faces turned to the sky. Then quietly they unlinked hands and filed away, followed by the spectators.

I realized that all through this encounter there had been no wind and there still wasn't. I looked up at a nondescript sky, an even grey. The stones were still pulsing, glowing with an ethereal light. I went to the trilith in the middle and stood, surveying the alignments. With no sun, no moon, no stars, it was a fruitless task. I put my arms around a pulsing stone and shut my eyes. I could feel an energy in it, tied to some-where beneath the ground. The stone was like a prism, focusing the energy, drawing it upwards and outwards. It was like being strapped to a rocket; a sudden rush of energy propelled me up into the sky. An unfamiliar landscape lay below; where my house was, there stood a long, low, thatched building; the henge was directly below me. There were no roads, no other houses. Forests stretched in all directions with the odd clearing scattered between them. Two of the clearings appeared to be tilled, another held tethered long-haired cattle.

A plume of smoke rose directly from the longhouse, nearly vertical in the still air. I saw a herd of huge elk in one clearing, the enormous antlers of the males clearly visible even from a height. I felt no fear, no exhilaration, just a sense of being an observer in a foreign land. I floated, arms and legs outspread, feeling the gentle passing of the air on my cheeks. I closed my eyes and wallowed in it, felt my spirits soar as my body had. When I opened my eyes again I was looking at the same dull sky, my back was pressed to the ground. I was in the field in front of my house, and there was no stone circle. The wind was blowing in gusts, my coat was wide open and I felt cold.

I walked back to the house and found Clair putting logs on the fire.

'Where the hell have you been? I had to bring in these logs myself.'

'If you want to burn them, you can carry them,' I said.

'Are you trying to be unpleasant?'

'No. Just fighting my corner.'

'Well I'm in no mood for fighting. I don't see why you expect me to do everything around here.'

'I don't. Do whatever you want for yourself, but don't do anything for me. I'll look after myself.'

I took off my coat and sat down in the armchair, waiting for her to have the last word, but she didn't. Didn't say a word, even when I slowly and deliberately rolled myself a cigarette and smoked it.

I thought about Pan. The great god, *Pan aeternum*. Bucolic

Pan, benevolent Pan. How did he ever become the Christian icon for the devil? Horns and cloven feet, once the symbols of the earth god, have become Satan's symbols. It's the legacy of Christianity; out with the old, in with the new. Like druids, like mushrooms; displaced, demonized, and fit only for outlanders like me.

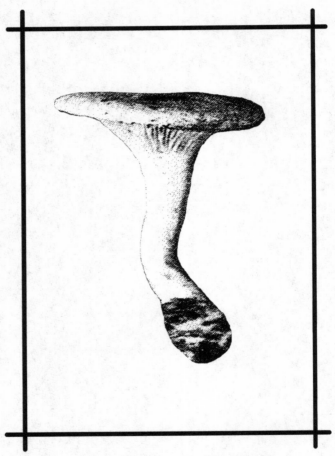

Hygrophoropsis aurantica. The False Chanterelle.
Cap 1-4 inches. Yellow to orange. Tough flesh.
Distinguished from chanterelle by lack of apricot smell.
Heaths and under conifers. Autumn.
Edible but might cause hallucinations.

eleven

I hadn't even begun to formulate my reply to the last two e-mails from the mushroom.man when yet another arrived. It was as though I'd opened a sluice-gate by simply asking for some everyday information. However, embedded in the rather mundane descriptions of people real or imaginary was more information relevant to my research. Not only that, but every disclosure made me feel that somehow our bond had become closer. To put it bluntly, the more he told me of his life the more influence I felt I had over him.

After this length of time and this much contact, albeit electronic, I felt increasingly sure of my position in his world. I had obviously become his confidante, someone to whom he was prepared to entrust a piece of his life. And that meant that to some extent I could guide him into giving me the information that I wanted to complete my paper. What I wanted after this was essentially more of the same. I needed to build up a picture of the man behind the e-mail before I could make good use of the information I had already garnered. Thankfully, he obliged without much prompting, reinforcing my belief that this contact with me was functioning as a kind of therapy for him.

Attn. mushroom.seeker.
Subject: more history.
9 September.

I hadn't seen Dave for nearly a year when he turned up one afternoon. He looked even thinner than usual and was very brown. Looking at him it was hard to believe this was a

Scotsman. Armenian, maybe. He sat down on the floor and made a half-hearted attempt to get into a full lotus. He settled into a half one and then assailed me.

'Just back from India, man.'

'Yeah?'

'Amazing. I mean fucking amazing. I went all over the place. I was up in the lakes of Kashmir and they'd blow your mind. I really got into the spiritual vibe, man. The Indians have really got it sussed.'

'Can't feed themselves, though.'

'Jesus, that's a material thing to say. That's just not what's happening there, man. Like these people are really amazing, they're not into all that western crap. They're just part of the flow, like it's all karma man, they're just part of it, know what I mean?'

'Yeah.'

'You'd really get off on it. It's such a spiritual thing. This whole western thing, man, it's crazy. We don't know how to empty our minds and just be at one with it all.'

'I know a few people with empty minds.'

'Very fucking funny. I'm serious, man. We've got a lot to learn from these guys. Like nothing fazes them, not even death. I've seen more dead and diseased bodies in the last year than you can imagine. It's weird, no one gives a shit. It's all down to karma. Shit, it's cold in here.'

I set about lighting the fire while Dave made tea. He came back with two mugs.

'I don't know how you take this weather. It's freezing. I only got back two days ago and I still haven't warmed up. Over there you can get by with just a tee-shirt. You don't need clothes, you don't need money.'

'Clair's been living here.'

'Yeah, I know.'

'Did she tell you?'

'Sort of, yeah.'

I waited for something more, but he seemed unwilling to talk.

'Do you mind her staying here?'

'Na. Look, I don't think I handled it very well. I just sort of split. Didn't tell her or anything. I just wanted to find myself, know what I mean?'

'Not really.'

'I just felt that we weren't really going anywhere. I needed a change. We both did. I mean I just felt there had to be more to it, yeah?'

'I suppose.'

'She's a great lady, you know? We had great times and that. Is she OK?'

'Well enough.'

'Great. I'm glad. Thanks for looking after her.'

'I'm not sure I have.'

'You know what I mean.'

I wanted to know just what Dave thought I had done for Clair. In my view of things Clair had done things entirely for herself, with me as an unwilling participant. Well, lately anyway. I also wanted to know just how much Dave had been a prime mover in Clair's coming to stay. Had he used me to salve his conscience? Or was it something they'd agreed between themselves? Dave got up to go to the loo. I fanned the flames of the fire and thought about what he'd said. Didn't need money in India. That's a joke. What was he doing there? Living on the charity of the world's poorest people? Him with tens of thousands of dollars, maybe even hundreds, sitting in offshore accounts. Money never seems important to those who have it.

He came back, stuffing a brass pot into his rucksack. Once again he tried and failed to sit in the lotus position. I couldn't shake off the thought that there was something absurd about this Pauline conversion. Probably the most venal person I'd ever met was telling me about mysticism. I decided to be charitable and take it at face value. Maybe he'd had a change of perspective. I've never been to India, but anyone I've met who has found it a humbling and moving experience. No reason why Dave should be any different.

Dave was rolling a joint and I took the mugs into the kitchen. The floor was covered in water. A trail of water led to the lavatory which was also covered in water – the seat and the floor. It looked as though someone had turned on a sprinkler system. I flushed it, and everything seemed to be working. Puzzling. I went back to Dave and found him lighting up.

'Was the loo leaking when you went?'

'No. Oh, did I splash a bit?'

'What?'

'Sorry, I might have splashed a bit.'

'I'm not following this.'

'No, it's just that I don't use paper any more. Wiping isn't hygienic. I have a pot of water instead. Wash instead of wipe. Don't sit down any more either, I squat on the seat. It's a much healthier position.'

An image formed in my mind of Dave squatting on the seat splashing himself and everything else with water, in the interests of hygiene.

'I see. Maybe another time you'd clear up afterwards.'

'Sure, man.'

I was grateful that Clair was out. I was hoping that before she came back I might have a better idea of what had happened between them. I don't think I could have dealt with this meeting had she been there. Things had become very strained between us.

'Did you tell Clair to come here?'

'Not really. But when she said she was thinking of it, I said it was a good idea.'

'Thanks.'

'I thought you'd get along OK.'

It occurred to me that here was my chance. Get Dave to take her back. That would solve everything. Brilliant.

'I suppose Clair will want to go back with you, now that you're back.'

'Dunno. Maybe.'

'Well what do you want?'

'Dunno. I might go back to India. Jesus, man, I fucked my

brains out there. Had more fucking women, Jesus it was great. Fucked myself silly.'

'Look, Dave, we're not really getting on very well, Clair and me.'

'No?'

'Not really. We had a big fight a couple of weeks ago.'

'What about?'

'A cat. A pregnant cat. This cat turned up and started hanging about the house. After a couple of weeks I realized it was pregnant, its belly got bigger and bigger. Anyway Clair's always leaving doors open and the cat kept coming into the house and pissing everywhere. She kept feeding it, and I kept chucking it out. It became obvious that soon I was going to have kittens as well pissing in the house, so I shot it.'

'Far out, man. Shot the fucking cat.'

'I shot it while Clair was out, but she met me on the lane. I had the cat in a bag and was going to dump it in the river. She must have guessed what was in the bag, because she grabbed it from me. When she saw what was in it she went for me, fists, nails, everything. She tried to bite me. Screaming at me. Anyway, we haven't really talked since then. Truth is we're not really compatible.'

'She doesn't fuck you, right?'

'No she doesn't, but that's not the point. It's a personality thing.'

'Yeah, sure. That's why I left, man. She'd just went off having sex. Made up for it in India, though.'

He winked and I could almost feel an elbow in my ribs. It was as if this had nothing to do with him any more. As far as he was concerned Clair was my responsibility now. Except she wasn't. She wasn't any man's chattel; she did what she liked whenever she wanted with no reference to me or anyone else. It was clear that however my problems with Clair were going to be resolved, Dave had nothing to do with it. It was between her and me.

Dusk was falling and I knew that Clair would be back soon. She'd be back for supper. Maybe it was a good thing that Dave was here; it wasn't just me and Clair who had stuff to work out.

We were looking at Dave's photographs when Clair walked in. There was a pile of them that he was particularly proud of devoted to women with no clothes on, mostly in hotel rooms. Hookers, I suspected. Dave gathered them up and put them in his jacket pocket, but not quickly enough. Clair noticed.

'Not for my eyes, eh?'

'Hi, Clair, good to see you.'

'Sure. Hi.' She walked off casually, as though Dave were of no consequence to her. He turned to me.

'She looks great.'

'Yeah, she does.'

He started talking me through the photographs of mountains and lakes in a loud voice, apparently oblivious to the fact that Clair had already understood what was in his pocket. He kept looking over his shoulder as he talked, as though expecting her to walk in at any moment and demand to see his holiday snaps. When I'd seen them all I went to look for Clair. Some of the photographs had disturbed me, the ones in the hotel rooms. Brown women posing lewdly, sometimes singly, sometimes in twos or threes. Faces of poverty, looking out at me, exploited and exploiting. Nothing very spiritual about sex tourism. But it was the twinges of envy that disturbed me. I found Clair in the bathroom combing her hair.

'Why don't you come in and join us?'

'I will, in a minute.'

'Right.'

Back in the sitting room I found Dave looking fretful. He was hopping about like a flea.

'Look, maybe this wasn't such a good idea, man. Maybe I should split.'

'Calm down. She'll be here in a minute.'

'I know, yeah.'

He sat down, and then almost immediately got up again. He walked around the room.

'Shit, it's cold.'

'Stand by the fire then.'

'Right.'

He stood, back to the grate, rubbing his hands. He knelt down and poked a log perfunctorily. He got up again and looked out the window.

'Nearly dark. I ought to go.'

'Relax. Sit down.'

He sat on the edge of the armchair, his knees hopping up and down. Clair walked in and sat opposite Dave.

'Well?'

'Great. Yeah, fine, OK. Bit cold.' He rubbed his hands.

'You bastard.'

'What?'

'You fucking bastard. You turn up here expecting every-thing to be like it was, as though nothing happened? You've been gone fourteen months, for fuck's sake.'

'Thirteen.'

'Fourteen. And what about me? Christ, you're a selfish bastard. Just fucked off and left me. How the hell do you expect me to feel?'

'Dunno. Sorry.'

'Is that it? Dunno, sorry? Jesus why don't you grow up. You're not a little boy. You've got responsibilities. I suppose you think I'm just going to come running, just because you're back.'

'No, not really.'

'Damn right I'm not. You can fuck off back to India for all I care.'

She started to cry. Quietly at first and then with more abandon. I'd never seen her cry before. Dave was making lit-tle twitchy movements, as though wanting to move to her side. I handed her a tea-towel. She held it to her face and sobbed. I couldn't think of anything to say, so I left the room and sat on my bed. What a mess. What a bloody mess. I lay down. I really had no idea how to handle this. I wanted her out of my house, but how could I do that to her now? I thought I could hear sounds of voices coming from the sitting-room, muffled and unclear. It was almost completely dark in the room now, as I tried to form some sort of plan. Perhaps I fell asleep. I remember the door opened, the light flooding in. I saw Clair silhouetted in the doorway.

'Can I come in?'

'Sure.'

She stood at the side of the bed and in the half light I saw she was totally naked.

'Can I get under the covers? It's cold out here.'

'Yeah, of course.'

I found that I was in the bed already. I had no recollection of getting in. Last thing I remembered was lying on top of the bed. She shivered.

'Hold me.'

I did. Held her close and tight.

'You OK?'

'Yeah.' She kissed my cheek. 'Thanks.'

She slid a knee between my thighs, her hand found my erection. It was more than a cuddle she wanted. Maybe she just wanted to feel needed, attractive. Dave had seemed pretty sure that he didn't want to go back to her.

'Dave gone?'

'Yup.'

I relaxed and let her take the lead. She'd always been so passive, so uninvolved. Yet here was the same woman, passionate and horny, really letting go. We made love for the first time; wild sex – sweaty sex. When she kissed me her tongue darted around my palate, teasing and exploring, her orgasms were explosive and so were mine. This was what I wanted, what I needed. Lying back afterwards I felt better than I'd felt for years. Clair had her head on my shoulder and cradled my limp dick in her hand. Her hair smelt wonderful, we were warm and comfortable. The world took on a new hue. I could live with this with ease. It was a revelation, I had no idea sex could be this good. Whatever her thoughts may have been, I went to sleep completely happy.

I woke up to an empty bed. In a panic I ran into the

kitchen. No one there. I called for her, called outside, ran around the house. I slowly realized all her things were gone. How could she do that, after last night? It had to have been as good for her as it was for me. Had to be. Then I saw the note on the table, propped up against a pot of marmalade.

'Sorry to go without saying good-bye. Dave asked me to go to London with him, and I'm going. Thanks for putting up with me, maybe we'll get the mill together one day. Best wishes, Clair.'

I stared at it stupidly, and then noticed there was more under my thumb. It said simply 'thanx, man, Dave.' I sat down and felt an overwhelming *déjà vu*. Women keep leaving me. Every time. But what was the sequence of events here? They'd both signed the note, so they were both here. Did I imagine last night? Dream it? There must be evidence. I went back to the bedroom and searched the bed carefully. I smelt the pillows, checked for hazel hair. I felt quite demented, I was searching for my sanity. Then I found a long hazel hair underneath the pillow. It did happen, then. She was here. But then where was Dave? If they left together he surely didn't wait while she came into my room and fucked my brains out. That made no sense. Unless that was the condition she set – a punishment for him. No, that was insane. When did I last change the sheets? Jesus, don't know. Maybe two weeks ago. Maybe more. This hair could have been there since then. In which case I could have imagined it all.

I went back and read the note again. There was no time written on it, just the message. Definitely Dave's writing, spidery, like a child's. I closed my eyes and tried to picture the events of last night. But still I remembered it as real, not as I remember dreams. Either way she was gone. Yesterday I would have been delighted, now I felt desolated. And yet, I reasoned to myself, if it was all in my imagination then I should feel no different than I did yesterday. Nothing had changed; only a fantasy had come and gone. But still it felt real. I sat at the table and cried for the loss of what might have been.

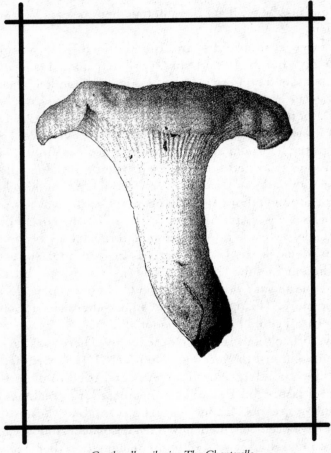

Cantharellus cibarius. The Chanterelle.
Cap 1-4 inches. Apricot to egg-yolk yellow.
Strong smell of apricots. Tender flesh.
Woodlands. Especially under deciduous trees in moss. Summer to Autumn.
Edible and excellent. A gourmet's delight.

twelve

I had, by this stage, come to accept what I received from the mushroom.-man as autobiographical. There seemed to be a good fit between what personal history he had told me and the philosophy that underpinned his way of dealing with the world. The two linked so nicely that it was easier to assume truth than artifice.

Even though the summer holidays were here, I remained living on the campus. A few summer courses were taking place, but it was largely empty. Even if I'd wanted to discuss my ideas about the mushroom.man with someone, there really was no one who I could talk to. The university was full of temporary staff and pupils; the few remaining regular staff were not the sort that I would have shared my research with, even had they had an interest.

What the long, warm summer gave me was the opportunity to organize my thoughts regarding the mushroom.man and my paper. What I most wanted to clarify were the two relationships that seemed to predominate in his life. On the surface his descriptions made those relationships seem essentially normal, but I wondered if further information might prove them to be dysfunctional, which would help my thesis. I felt sufficiently secure in my role as confidante that I felt I could ask a personal question directly.

I sent this short e-mail:

Attn. mushroom.man.
Subject: more questions.
11 September.

I know I keep pestering you for information about you and your life, but it intrigues me. Two elements occur regularly: you relationship with Greg and your relationship with Jane. Both of these are in the past. I would agree that history shapes our present, but as an observer I would say that you appear overly preoccupied with events in the past. Do you think that's fair? Let me know.

I got my reply soon after.

Attn. mushroom.seeker.
Subject: more history.
15 September.

Not long ago I got a postcard of Tower Bridge, an enhanced colour tourist job. It was from Jane. Just a short note saying she'd be over for a week or two and that she wanted to see me. No address, no dates. Some days later a phone call. She'd hired a car and was coming that afternoon. Just like that; very efficient, almost formal. I didn't know what to expect. Nine years can be a long time.

I heard the car in the lane and went out to greet her. She stepped out and stood still, looking at me and the cottage. I saw the woman I remembered, but with short, bobbed hair, a tailored suit and high heels. She picked her way across the muddy yard carefully, staring at the ground. She reached me and looked up.

'I'd forgotten how much mud there is here. You're looking well.'

'So are you.'

'Can we go in?'

'Of course, yes, sorry.'

We went in and she casually draped her jacket over the back of the sofa, label exposed. I think she expected the label to mean something to me, but it didn't. She looked around.

'Hasn't changed much.'

'Suppose not.'

'Same furniture.'

'Yes.'

We'd bought it at a house auction. The sofa was the first and only that I'd ever bought. It wasn't in great condition then – now I saw it with her eyes. It had a definite touch of tat to it.

'Are you here for long?'

'Just a fortnight. I got the urge to look up old friends. See how everyone was doing.'

'I see.'

'So how are you?'

'Fine. Well enough. You know. It's not a whole lot different than when you, um, than when you went away.'

'I can see that.' She smiled what seemed a genuinely affectionate smile. 'Any chance of a cup of tea?'

'Of course, sorry, I should have thought of that. I'll make some.'

She followed me into the kitchen and watched while I got the tea ready. Funny; I remembered a young woman, a woman with a young girl's personality, and here was a mature Jane, confident, poised and elegant. That's it, I thought, she's elegant. That's the difference. The years had treated her well, she looked better now than she ever had while living with me. Perhaps that was the problem – she couldn't thrive with me. She looked great. I turned to her.

'You look really well.'

'Thanks.' She looked around the kitchen. 'I see you're still growing mushrooms.'

'Oh, them. Yes, occasionally.'

We sat down and were silent for a moment. The clinks of the cups and saucers seemed loud. It began to rain, the wind spattering the drops against the windows. She looked out.

'Quite like old times.'

'Yeah, still raining.'

I was trying not to voice the question that hung in the air. What are you here for? Why do you want to see me? I thought it better to wait and let her tell me in her own time. Assuming she would.

'So have you seen many of the old gang?'

'A few, yes. Nothing much changes here, does it? I mean everyone just seems to go on as they always did. Funny.'

'You have kids now, don't you?'

'Two, yes. Toby is seven and Ophelia is four.'

'Are they with you?'

'No, they're staying with their father. While I'm here.'

Staying with their father. Has a ring of divorce to it, or separation. Not 'they're at home', no; staying with their father. Not with Bob or Bill or whatever his name is. Their father. Puts a bit of distance between them.

'So what are your plans? Can you stay for supper?'

'I'd love to, yes. No plans in particular. Just taking each day as it comes.'

'Great. Fancy a walk?'

'In this rain?'

'I'll lend you a coat and wellies. It's not heavy rain, it'll do us good to get out a bit.'

'OK, I'll come, but I'm not enthusiastic.'

It wasn't as bad outside as it seemed from inside. There was a bit of rain, but it was more like a fine mist. Gentle. We took one of our old walks, up through the forest to the top of the hill. There's a big granite erratic sitting there, with a ledge on one side like a bench. We sat there and took in the view. Jane dried her face with a handkerchief. For a moment I thought she'd been crying. We talked of trees, seasons and birds. A bit like a nature walk – we touched on nothing personal. On the way back we stopped at the bridge and played Pooh sticks, just like years ago. We were laughing and giggling like children, running from one side of the bridge to the other, shouting, squealing, playing. I felt great, comfortable with her, even happy.

We went home slowly, chatting of nothing in particular, both of us avoiding any topic that might hurt. I still had no idea of why she was here, but I was sure she'd tell me when the time was right. I thought of telling her about the stone circle, but didn't. When we got home I lit a fire and left her to warm up. I went into the kitchen to see if I could make good my offer of supper. Rabbit, that was about it. Well, rabbit or nothing actually. I shouted out: 'Rabbit OK with you?'

She walked in. 'Done how?'

'I dunno. Mustard sauce?'

'Lovely. Want some help?'

'Sure. Glad of the company.'

I've never been good at dealing with old lovers. Maybe I'm not civilized enough. But I felt happy that evening being with Jane. Time buries the hurt. We were like old friends, comfortable in each other's company, playing no silly games. I had a couple of bottles of wine and we drank them both over the course of the meal. Quite like old times, I thought. Two things were on my mind; I still wanted to know what had prompted this visit, and I wanted her to stay the night – I wanted to see her the next day.

'So, are you enjoying your visit?'

'It's great to be back. I'd forgotten how much fun it is here. It's a different world in London.'

'Yeah?'

'It's more intense there, I think. There doesn't seem to be as much time for play. I mean when I went there I thought 'I'm moving to the big city; lots of people', but you end up living in your own little village inside it. I probably know fewer people by name than I did here.'

'Worlds within worlds.'

'Exactly. It turned out to be quite a small world in the end. There's work and home – I work in a shop selling terracotta and ceramics, all hand-made – and then home. The usual, you know, cooking, cleaning, getting the kids to school. You never met Theo, but he's very self-obsessed. For him work and life are one and the same thing.'

'What does he do?'

'He runs his own ad agency now. Very well thought of. Berry and Hartley. It takes up all his time.'

'Presumably well rewarded.'

'Oh yes. Very. It's just that, well, oh I don't know. I don't want to bore you with all that.'

'It's not boring. I want to hear it.'

She studied the table, then she looked up at me.

'I don't really believe that money is all that matters.'

'Who the fuck does?'

'Theo does. It's all he ever thinks about. He's very good to us, gives me plenty of money, but it's almost as though he's just buying a family, do you know what I mean?'

'I think so.'

'Instead of time and effort he puts in money. I shouldn't complain, I'm luckier than most.'

'In what way?'

'Well, I have two great kids, I'm healthy, they're healthy, we live in a nice house. It's what a lot of people dream of. Anyway, enough of me. What about you? What are you doing?'

'Much the same, really. I feel like I've been walking down this untrodden path for years now and it still hasn't led me anywhere. But I just go on believing that it will. That there's a destination at the end waiting to be discovered. All the things I do day to day are just to let me go on exploring. I don't suppose that makes much sense.'

'Oh, it does. You're still chasing those worlds in your head. The same ones you never let me be a part of.'

'Ah, Jane. Is that what you thought? What a crazy world this is. I always thought you weren't interested.'

Maybe that's why I always end up alone. Two minds, two parallel worlds. You never know what anyone else really thinks or wants. How do you communicate an internal vision? What words can you use when there are none to describe it? Jane's world and mine were no longer even parallel; they'd become divergent. A world of schools, children and responsibilities; different from mine. Yet there must be points of common reference. Whatever she hadn't shared with me, there was a lot that she had. We knew each other well. I wanted her to stay, at least for another day.

We sat over coffee, talking about the people we had known, what they were doing with their lives. She was, she said, curious as to how their lives had turned out. I suspected that she wanted a scale against which to measure hers. Eventually I asked.

'So, does Theo know that you're here?'

'Yes, of course. He knows about you; I've talked to him about life here. I think he's rather pleased to get rid of me for a bit.'

'What about your kids?'

'I imagine he'll just let the nanny do everything. He won't get involved. I don't know, maybe a break will do us both good.'

'Would you like to stay here tonight? I mean not with me – I'll sleep on the sofa. Just so you don't have to go back in the dark.'

'I don't know if I should.'

'No pressure. It would be nice to spend some more time with you. I've really enjoyed seeing you again. We could go out riding tomorrow, if you'd like.'

'God, I haven't been riding for years. You know, I think I'd like that.'

'Great. It'll be fun.'

It was a relief to know I'd have the next day to talk to her. I wanted to know more about her life, and above all what had made her come to visit. I also wanted to tell her about the stones and my strange vision of Greg and her. I'd spoken to no one about it, and I wanted to. I remember desperately trying to clear up my bedroom while Jane went into the bathroom. Stuffing clothes into drawers, picking up socks, tidying as best I could. She walked in just as I realized the sheets hadn't been changed for ages. I pulled them off and rolled them up before she could see them too well. Between us we laid clean sheets. It occurred to me that since I wasn't going to wash the old ones right away, they'd do to make the sofa comfortable.

I lay on the sofa watching the dying flames in the hearth. I fantasized briefly of Jane in my bed, and then went to sleep.

Next morning she wakened me with a cup of coffee and pulled back the curtains. Nice that she felt she could make herself at home. I sat up swaddled in bedding.

'Funny to be back in this house. Hasn't changed much.'

'No. Good to see you, Jane.'

'You too.'

We sat quietly, sipping our coffees. I was waking up little by little, taking in the morning light. It was an odd feeling, seeing Jane sitting there. It was almost as though the last nine years had never happened. I began thinking about friendship. I'd never had a woman friend who wasn't a lover. Or if I had, it was because I was hoping for more. Never had the sort of friendship I'd had with Greg. I was wondering whether this was a shortcoming in me or the natural state of things when Jane spoke.

'I've been thinking.'

'Yeah?'

'About the past – about us.'

'And?'

'I was just thinking that, you know, we never really had a chance to talk about what happened. To us, I mean.'

'I know.'

'And I was thinking that maybe I owe you an explanation.'

'You don't have to.'

'Maybe not. But I just feel a lot went unsaid.'

'Just about everything.'

'I think we wanted different things from life. I really wanted children.'

'You never said.'

'I just felt that it was something you weren't prepared for. You were very much a child yourself, I could never see you as a father.'

'I see. And Theo fits the bill, does he?'

'Don't be cross. I'm just trying to explain.'

'Sorry.'

'I really thought he did, yes. The classic provider. Someone who could give my children a good start. I'm not sure here is the best place for children to grow up. God, that doesn't sound right, but you know what I mean. I'm not explaining this very well.'

'Biological imperative.'

'What?'

'I understand. You wanted kids and you wanted the best nest that you could find. Whatever else, I've learnt about my own shortcomings over the years. You know, I don't think I can even count the number of women who've left me in the last nine years. It's got to the stage that I expect it.'

'That sounds awful.'

'It's not supposed to. Just a statement of fact.'

'Maybe there's no room for anyone else where you're going.'

'Maybe not.'

While I got dressed Jane went out for a walk. Truth is strange; it's liberating and at the same time depressing. Depressing because once exposed, all the comforting fantasies that were there in its place have to go. Cold reality is left. The sort of reality that says a leaking roof and mould is not for my children. That's a judgement based on cool appraisal. She was right. In many ways I've lived like a child, never planning for the future; not so much avoiding responsibility as simply never assuming it. I had never thought of myself as poor, but suddenly I saw my house, my way of life, in a new light. Maybe it really was seedy and run down. Maybe it mattered. *Oh wad some power the giftie gie us to see oursels as others see us!*

I got a sudden urge to tidy the house. It was disheartening; the more I started to clean and tidy the more I could see that needed doing. I became more manically thorough than I'd ever been. I took rugs outside and shook them, puffed up

cushions, made tidy piles of things on surfaces. It was beginning to look presentable when I looked up at the ceiling. A
whole world of cobwebs and dust trembled lightly in the air.
By the time I'd removed as much as the brush could reach
every surface was covered in black specks of stuff and needed another going over. Paint, that was the answer. I'd have to
get some. The more I looked, the more tatty the view. I got it
into my head that I had to be finished before Jane came
back. God knows why. When she came back the air was
thick with disturbed dust.

'You've been busy.'

'I know. I just thought it was about time.'

'Too right.'

She looked impressed, probably not at the results, but at
the unaccustomed attempts at housework. There I go again,
I thought, doing things just to make an impression on a
woman. Maybe that's the only reason men ever do anything.

Keen to continue to be viewed in a favourable light I
offered Jane an early lunch of omelette. There were four
eggs in the hen house when I went out for them. Enough. I
thought Jane was a little fidgety over lunch, but I didn't
mention it. Eventually she took a deep breath and began.

'I suppose I might as well tell you, you've probably guessed
anyway. Things aren't really good between me and Theo.'

'No?'

'Haven't been for a while. I never see him, he's always
working. I never wanted to bring up my kids all alone, I did-
n't want to be a single mother.'

'I see.'

'Do you? The truth is I don't have any real friends. Just
people I meet through work, or some of the people that Theo
brings home. Sometimes I feel really lonely.'

'I'm sorry.'

'Don't be. I'm just being self-indulgent. It's not all that
bad really. I just wanted to tell someone, that's all. Funny
isn't it, how we go back to our past when things get hard.'

'What'll you do?'

'Do? Nothing, I suppose. I mean, when you think about it, doing something is such an upheaval for everyone that's it's easier to do nothing, isn't it?'

'Suppose so.'

'I'm sorry. It's not really fair of me to dump this on you.'

'It's OK, really. That's what friends are for, isn't it?'

I reached across the table and squeezed her hand. She smiled and squeezed back. It was becoming clear to me why she'd come. Hope. Hope that she might find something changed, something new. I wasn't fit to look after myself, let alone some other man's kids. I could hardly imagine having any of my own. But then again, I couldn't really trust my perceptions of people and their motives. Didn't have much of a track record of getting it right. This was probably another one of those fantasies that had validity only for me. It began to feel oppressive sitting in the half light of the kitchen. I felt the urge to get outside.

'Do you still feel like going riding?'

'Not really, if you don't mind. I should really be thinking about going back.'

'So soon?'

'Well in a while, anyway.'

'Come out to the field with me.'

'Why?'

'I want to show you something.'

I'd been thinking about how to approach this. If she was going to go soon it would have to be now. I was going to tell her about the stones and what I'd seen there – when I'd seen her and Greg. I had to know if there was any truth in it, if there was anything real, objectively true. Increasingly I was unsure if I was really meeting people or not. Sometimes I was, sometimes it was all imagined, sometimes I couldn't tell the difference. I wanted Jane to be my touchstone on reality once again.

Out in the field I showed her the huge boulders in the

surrounding walls. I told her about the map, and how circles had often been dismantled. And then I told her about my vision.

'Greg told me that we lived in more than one place and reality at a time. That I'd slipped into a parallel life with the consciousness of another. Does that make any sense?'

'Not a lot.'

'He told me he loved you.'

'Did he.'

'That he always did. Had.'

'And?'

'That's it.'

'I see. So what's the question?'

'There isn't one. I just wanted to know if it made any sense to you. I get confused sometimes.'

'Sounds to me like another drug-induced fantasy. You never learn, do you?'

I suppose it's unreasonable to expect people to bare their souls. I'm happy enough to do it, but I'm beginning to think most people aren't. I just hoped that in that moment Jane would tell me what I wanted to hear. That these were not fantasies but slices of reality; that she was there too in the circle, in a dream or in her imagination; that my description of the event was accurate. I wanted to hear her say, 'Yes, that's right, that's how it happened in my dream.' Then I would know; I would be sure that there was something real in the mushroom world. Instead I was no better off. I still had no evidence that any of these dreams had reality in them. But I still believed they did. I was sure that Jane simply didn't want to confirm it; that she could have, but chose not to. That it was fear on her part that made her refuse to corroborate my vision. Fear of accepting the reality of dreams.

Jane started walking back toward the house quickly. Grudgingly I fell into step.

'I have to go now. Thanks for dinner and everything.'

'That's OK.'

'I'll be in touch.'

'OK, great. Drive safely.'

She kissed me briefly on the cheek and got into the car. I watched her drive off. Such a sudden goodbye, so quick. Almost a dash for freedom. Was it really so horrid an idea, life with me?'

Langermannia gigantea. The Giant Puffball.
Large. To 30 inches in diameter. White. Skin leathery.
Strong mushroomy smell. Firm flesh.
On well-manured grass-lands. Late summer to late autumn.
Edible. Good sliced and fried.

thirteen

The last e-mail hadn't really answered my questions, so I reverted to my previous line of enquiry, that of looking for information as to how he filled his days.

One thing I had learned: the mushroom.man never answered anything directly. I had to be oblique in my questioning; directness appeared to be completely ignored. Yet when I looked back at what I had already received there was already a corpus of ideas that went a long way towards filling the gaps in my research.

It was around this time that something occurred to me. He had never asked anything of me. No questions of any kind. I wondered for a while if this was in any way insulting. I realized that although we had not had what might generally be regarded as a conversation, it was most certainly almost entirely one-sided. Not only that, but he had never made any reference at all to my e-mails to him. He responded, sometimes answering queries in a roundabout way, but never as a letter-writer might — never replying point by point or even mentioning what he'd received from me. Each one of my e-mails simply elicited a response, but somehow it wasn't a personal one, there was always a distance.

I decided to make no reference to this, as I really didn't want any complaint of mine to interrupt the flow of mail from him. I simply asked him to tell me a little about who he met and interacted with in the present, as opposed to the past.

Attn. mushroom.seeker.
Subject: hill walks.
22 September.

Two years went by before I heard from Hartfield Stanley again. I heard plenty about him in local gossip and saw his car on the road from time to time, but he had never asked me to his house again. Perhaps he was waiting for me to return his hospitality.

His latest venture was deer farming, breeding and raising Sika deer for the German market. There had been a fair bit of poaching over the past year and I had rather guiltily eaten some of his venison, passed on to me by a poacher. I thought of him from time to time, and of the two strange women who shared his house. I had assumed when I met them first that Yelena was just visiting, but she was still there, two years on. The same questions continued to niggle at me: was my vision of the women true? Did they really know Greg, or was that a figment of fantasy? I suppose I had let time pass because deep down I didn't really want to know the answer. No, that's not right. I didn't want to discover that my visions held no truth, so rather than risk that I avoided finding out. Still, it was something that was always at the back of my mind. If I could just once verify a part of a vision, my world would make more sense. I would really be discovering truth, not simply hallucinating.

So when I got a phone call from Hartfield asking me to come and see him, my reactions were mixed. Part of me wanted to keep my thoughts safe from change, while another part longed for verification. For two days I tried to think of a reason not to go, but eventually the time was up, and I had no excuse. I was to meet him at eleven, for a cup of coffee he had said, so at half-past ten I set off to walk to his place. In the two years since I had been there it had changed. Nothing major, no new buildings or extensions, just a lot of polish. As I walked up the drive everything shone. New post and rail fencing, raked gravel with not a blade of grass peeking through, beautifully mown lawns and perfect flower beds. The house had had the brick re-pointed and the stonework sandblasted. The eaves gleamed with fresh white paint, the chimney stacks too. As I arrived at the door I noticed all the windows had been double-glazed, but carefully enough; a casual glance and they looked as they always had.

Hartfield opened the door himself, greeted me warmly and took me into his study. The house was warm, far warmer than I was used to. He asked me to sit while he picked up the phone and said we'd take coffee in the morning room. We talked of the weather, we talked of horses. When the coffee came, carried in by his butler, he sat down in a chair beside me and poured for us both.

'Do you still take people on nature walks?'

'Occasionally, yes.'

'Good.'

He passed me a cup.

'Arabica. The best. Don't spoil it with sugar.'

'OK.'

'I was hoping you could help me.'

'I'll try.'

'I know I don't know you very well, but I'll be straight with you. I'm sure you remember White Cloud and Elena?'

'Yelena?'

'Yes. Well, frankly I think they're bored. Both of them had small falls out riding and they've gone off it now. They spend most of their time running into the city to do God knows what. Shopping, I suppose. That's where they are now. Fact is, I think if they don't get some kind of interest in this place, they're going to start pushing me to leave, and frankly I don't want to. I like it here, for the first time in my life I feel I've got roots. Does that make any sense to you?'

'Yes, I think so.'

'So can you help?'

'What do you want me to do?'

'Teach them about the countryside. Try and get them interested. Give them a reason for staying.'

'I can try.'

'Good. More coffee?'

He was the model of courtesy. He apologized for letting so much time pass before getting in contact. He hoped that now we had re-established our acquaintance we'd see a lot more of each other. He rose and moved toward the door.

'I'll be in touch.' He shook my hand and led me the front door. He looked out at the empty car park. 'Did you walk here?'

'Yes, I did.'

'Well that's great. Live as you preach.'

The enormity of what he had asked began to dawn on me as I walked home. He was asking me to take responsibility for his remaining here – putting his future in my hands. Well, that's a bit strong; no, I was just his first salvo. And I had agreed.

It meant facing some unpleasant thoughts. Suppose, I thought, that my vision of these women at the henge was a slice of truth. Then Yelena really did know about my sexual fantasies. I wasn't sure that I wanted that to be true. I didn't really like her, didn't relish her knowing things about me. It made me vulnerable, and I didn't like the thought of it.

A few days later Hartfield called me again. He wanted to walk to the top of Jack's Lug, the highest of the nearby hills. Would I accompany him and the two women? I said I would.

When I met them they were standing outside Hartfield's house wearing jeans and trainers. Both Yelena and White Cloud greeted me politely, and neither made any comment about meeting again. I made them change into heavy boots and carry, if not wear, wind-proof jackets. I don't think they believed me when I explained how cold it gets on exposed hillsides. The weather can close in frighteningly fast, even in the summer. You have to be prepared. As I was explaining this, Hartfield went to answer the phone. When he came out he looked apologetic.

'I'm sorry, you'll have to go without me. My agent just

called, and he's to call back in an hour or two. I'll have to stay.'

White Cloud looked at him coldly. 'Why didn't you tell Tony to call tonight?'

'Sorry. This won't wait. Go on without me. I'll come next time.'

'What next time?' White Cloud kicked at the gravel peevishly.

Yelena took the situation by the scruff. 'Hartfield doesn't have to come. We can go even if he needs to sit by a phone. Come on.'

She set off down the drive. Hartfield shrugged and started to go in.

Yelena turned back and called, 'Come on. If we don't go now there won't be enough time before the light goes. Come on.'

We walked in silence. I tried to keep the pace slow, since we had to conserve our energy. It was a long walk just to get to Jack's Lug, and then a fair climb to the summit. As we walked I found myself going through my usual speeches and talks almost on autopilot. Neither of the women said much, and they didn't really give me the impression they were listening either. They seemed immersed in their own world. It didn't seem like long before we had begun the climb up Jack's Lug. I was leading them up the easiest route, though not the shortest. About halfway up they put on their jackets. A brisk wind was blowing steadily, and we were now above the forestry with nothing to break the wind. The Lug doesn't really have a summit; there's a large flat area at the top covered in briars and furze. We found a clearing and sat. I took out my tobacco and rolled a cigarette.

'Smoking will kill you,' said Yelena.

'The alternative is not immortality.'

'Yes it is.'

'What?'

'Immortality is the alternative.'

'Are you saying that if I gave up smoking I'd live forever?'

177

'No. You'd have to do other things as well, but giving up tobacco would be a priority.'

White Cloud, who had been staring into the valley where Hartfield's house could just be seen, turned around.

'We are both immortal.'

'In what sense?'

'In the sense that we won't die, of course.'

'You mean your souls?'

'No, our bodies.'

They both looked so earnest that I managed to overcome a strong urge to laugh. Someone looks you straight in the eye and says unflinchingly, 'I'm immortal.' For God's sake, it's insane. Death is the only thing I'm certain of, and these two are telling me they'll live forever. Jesus.

'I don't think he believes us.'

'Well it's a little startling.'

'We belong to the Church of the Immortals. We have done for years.'

'How many? A hundred?'

'Don't be flippant. It's been ten years since we discovered The Way. It will bring enlightenment and immortality to all who believe.'

'So none of your church members die?'

'Some do.'

'I see.'

'But only those who fail. Not all our members really believe. The Way only brings you enlightenment and immortality if you truly believe.'

'So if anyone dies it's not because the teaching isn't true, it's because they're not following it properly. Is that it?'

'Absolutely.'

Perhaps this is no more insane than some of the stuff I believe in, I thought. And just about as elusive of objective proof. It's only a step away from believing in the immortality of the soul. That's a bit hard to prove as well.

'Is there a leader of this church? A guru?'

'We follow the teachings of Joe Kay and Jerry Konstad. They founded the Church back in the seventies.'

'How old are they?'

'Jerry is fifty-three years old. Joe left us for another place nine years ago.'

'He died?'

'No. He went to spread The Way in another place. A parallel world. He had to leave his body here to do that.'

'I see.'

'I doubt you do.'

'Look, the only kind of immortality that I can conceive of is if you were to connect your mind to a computer and download all its contents; memories, experiences, language. Store it, and then when the body dies load a clone's brain with the stored experiences. You live again; the same you in a different body. But even this way you're subject to proton decay — you can only survive as long as your storage medium. It's not quite immortality.'

I said no more. It occurred to me that if I could believe in the fantastic, then why shouldn't other people? I was never going to find room for this way of thinking in my own world view, but I wasn't going to knock it either. Not if it made them happy. The three of us just sat there, saying nothing, scanning the horizon. Eventually I broke the silence.

'Did either of you ever know a Greg?'

'Greg Binvek?'

'No, Holder.'

'Greg Holder. No, I don't think so. Do you, Yelena?'

'No. Does he live near here?'

'No, he's dead now. He was a friend of mine. He lived in California.'

'I was in California once. Went to a seminar on The Way in Sacramento. You were there too, weren't you Yelena?'

'Yup.'

'So you never met him?'

'Don't think so. Is it important?'

'No. Just wondered. We should start getting back. Sun's going down.'

Yelena lay back and stretched. She turned to me and smiled. 'You want to fuck me?'

'What?'

'You know, fucky-fucky. Would you like that?'

White Cloud turned to me. 'You can if you want. She'd like that. She's a horny little bitch. I won't look if you don't want me to.'

They both began to laugh. 'I think he's embarrassed – look, he's blushing, Yelena.'

'I'm sorry, I didn't mean to embarrass you. It's so nice and soft on the heather, I thought you might like to do it right here, in the open. I know the thought's crossed your mind.'

'What? I mean, how did you know that?'

'So it has crossed your mind.' She grinned slyly.

'I didn't say that. Anyway, we should be going. It'll be dark soon.'

Yelena sat up and shook her hair. 'How very sensible of you. Anyway, the offer still stands even if all you want to do is talk about proton decay.'

White Cloud and Yelena moved off quickly, arm in arm, talking, but I couldn't make it out. I got up and rubbed the dead bracken from my clothes. Clearly they'd been teasing me, but I still wondered if she really had read my thoughts.

A near full moon was rising in the east, just over the brow of a distant hill. Huge and cheesy, it made a spectacular moonrise. By the time we got to the bottom of the hill Venus was bright in the southern sky. Neither woman showed any sign of flagging. Immortal or not, they were certainly fit.

I left them at the drive to their house. I wanted to get home. I suggested another walk the next week, and was surprised when they agreed. I walked slowly, going over what they'd said. The name Joe Kay bothered me. I knew the name, but from where? Joseph K. Of course. Someone with a sense of humour had picked himself a *nomme de guerre*. Died nine years ago. Left for another place, whatever that means.

Was it Greg? It was possible.

Back home I sat with the lights off. Moonlight flooded through the windows, bright enough to see by. It was an irresistible light. I put on my jacket and walked outside, toward the henge. I saw it in the moonlight, as real, as tangible as anything else. I touched the stones, letting my fingers explore their every crevice, feeling their massiveness, their coldness. I sat on the wet grass, my back against the central trilith. It was soft, giving, like an armchair. I turned and touched it. It was warm, like flesh. I moved and the moonlight caught it in full. An enormous face in the stone. Greg's face. I felt his cheeks, his lips, touched the eyes. The eyes opened.

'Greg?'

'I hear you.'

'What's going on?'

'I'm going back, old buddy. Back to the earth. For a while I floated like you, on the surface, now I'm going back to be a part of it again.'

'I don't understand.'

'Of course you do. You always say that when you can't think of anything else to say. It's a meaningless mantra.'

'Can I ask you a question?'

'What?'

'Are any of these visions real?'

'Look at the moon.'

I turned to look at it. High in the sky now, it had lost its yellowness and had shrunk back to its normal size. Thin cloud high up gave it a halo, I was sure I could see a moonbow. It was so bright that no stars were visible anywhere near it. I turned back to the stone. The face was gone. I touched it; it was hard and cold. Did I imagine the face? I started to laugh. Absurd. Of course I had imagined it, I was imagining these stones. They weren't here, they didn't exist. They were lying on their sides in the ditch, not standing here casting shadows in the moonlight.

I walked to the ditch, to where I knew at least two stones were. I could make them out in the moonlight, part of the wall, as I knew they should be. I looked back toward my house and the henge was gone. Just as it should be. Slowly I made my way back, enjoying the bright night. I was in front of the house when headlights shone up my lane. A car pulled in, a large and shiny one. It was Hartfield. He got out and came up to me.

'So this is where you live. Very nice.'

'You're welcome. Come on in. I was just out walking.'

'Sucker for punishment, eh?'

'Suppose so.'

'I'll just call the girls.'

He went back to the car and opened the doors. White Cloud and Yelena got out, still dressed in their walking clothes. They walked in, making much of wiping their feet on the mat.

'Neat place,' said Yelena.

'Thanks. Would you like a drink? I've got some beer.'

'Not for me. Got any mint tea?'

'I've got some mint growing outside. That OK?'

'Sure.'

'I'll have some too,' said White Cloud.

'Beer for me,' said Hartfield.

I got Hartfield a beer and then went out to pick the mint. When I came back the women were looking at a photograph on the wall of Greg, Jane and me.

'Who's this?'

'Jane. She used to live here with me.'

'And this?'

'An old friend of mine. Greg Holder.'

When I think back on this moment I'm sure that the two women exchanged a glance. Maybe not, but I think they did. Yelena put the photo back on the wall. As she raised her arms, I saw damp sweat marks.

'She's pretty.'

'Yes.'

I made the tea and while we sipped our drinks I waited to hear the purpose of the visit. Hartfield began.

'The girls think you might be interested in some news.'

'Yeah?'

'Tell him, White Cloud.'

'OK. Remember I told you about the Church of the Immortals this afternoon? Well Jerry Konstad is coming here. Next week in fact, to our church. We thought maybe you'd like to come.'

'Oh. Right. Yeah, that might be interesting. Sure.'

Strange. Did they really need to come here to tell me that? A phone call would have done. Don't see them for two years, then twice in the same day. Hartfield got up abruptly.

'Thanks for the beer. We'll leave you to it. Girls.'

Before I'd got my thoughts into order they'd gone. I watched Hartfield negotiate the potholes on the lane until I could no longer hear the car. I sat in my favourite chair and enjoyed the silence. Far away a nightjar called.

Connections. Real or imaginary? I tried to analyse them, tried to ascertain if my perceptions of connections running through my life were actual, or whether they were a product of my wish to find them. The first problem I had to deal with was conceit. Was it really possible that this odd group of people that had affected my life were entangled because of me? Unlikely, surely. If I were honest with myself I could see that my life was uneventful, fruitless, and possibly purposeless. Given that, why should anyone's destiny be linked to mine? Jane through Greg, Clair through Dave and some ley-line. White Cloud and Yelena through Greg. Or maybe not. I might have imagined the last one. A turbulent picture of links real and imagined. Maybe the only reason they appear to be connected to me is because that's where I see it from. My point of view; an egocentric universe.

A maxim of Cicero came to mind. *Veræ amicitiæ sempiternæ sunt*, real friendships are forever. Maybe that was the point. What defines friendship is the binding of destinies together. Once linked, the bond is forever. Across the years, across realities, maybe even across lives.

Amanita phalloides. The Death Cap.
Cap 2-6 inches. White with white gills. Smells of potatoes.
Recognised by ring on stem and egg-like base.
In deciduous woods, occasionally coniferous, especially under oak.
Summer to early autumn.
Virulently poisonous, kills by destroying liver and kidneys.
No antidote after symptoms appear.

fourteen

This last message pleased me more than any other that I'd got from the mushroom.man. He had finally acknowledged, however tangentially, something that I had written. He had responded to my assertion that he dwelt almost to the point of pathological intensity on his relationships with Greg and Jane — although I hadn't put it as strongly as that. He had also described his interactions with people in the present sufficiently for me to get a real impression of his interpersonal relationships.

By any standards this was real progress. What could well have been described as two sequential monologues was verging on becoming a dialogue. Well, perhaps not completely. There was still the difference that asynchronicity makes to a dialogue. It was a dialogue with no grace-notes, no spontaneous asides. But that was dictated by the format of the exchange, not by individual volition. I felt as if we had been singing two different melodies in different rhythms, and that now they were somehow moving into phase.

I really believed that we had crossed some kind of Rubicon; or rather he had. Whatever had first prompted him to correspond with me, now his motivation appeared to be the content of my e-mails. I was sure now that the stratagems I had pursued were apt to the task and had shown themselves to be effective. I resisted the temptation to be totally direct from now on, but the thrust of my enquiries became more invasive.

By the end of September preparations for the new university term were under way. I wanted to have the bulk of my research completed soon, leaving me free to devote my energies to my job rather than to the peculiar relationship I had developed with the mushroom.man. So in the hope of learning more of what I wanted to know I sent him this:

Attn. mushroom.man.
Subject: philosophy.
27 September.

Tell me this. I understand that your attachment to the daily world is as tenuous as you can make it whilst keeping body and soul together. However, you presumably have some kind of rationale that dictates the hows and the whys. You've made it plain that you don't take mushrooms for recreation, only for exploration, and I accept that. What I don't know is why you do it. Where do you think it'll lead? I'd be grateful if you could try to answer that.

That was about as direct as I was prepared to be. He could be evasive if he wished, but with such direct questions it would be an obvious evasion. I was sure that he would give me some kind of reply based on my questions. I was so sure of it that I began collating and organizing everything he'd sent me in preparation for the first draft of my paper. I had my answer in a few days.

Attn. mushroom.seeker.
Subject: immortality.
2 October.

I was preparing Petri plates when the phone rang. It was Hartfield and he wanted me to come to his house that afternoon. I had no reason to refuse, so I accepted. Also I was curious about the Church of the Immortals. He didn't say as much, but I was sure that was the reason for the call.

I'd been thinking about this idea of immortality as a sort of prize for living well. I couldn't take it seriously and anyway, I was by no means sure that I wanted to live forever. Not if it meant giving up tobacco.

It all depends on how you perceive death. If you sanctify life then you have to demonize death, since it puts an end to a state of sanctity. Yet as far as we are aware it is unavoidable and therefore our state of sanctity is temporary. Preserving sanctity means postponing death for as long as possible. And yet most religions insist that a better state awaits after death. Valhalla, heaven, nirvana are supposed by many to be a better place. If that's true then perhaps we should be rushing toward our death rather than seeking to avoid it.

I can't help believing that life and death are like light and dark. One state is dependent upon the other. They can't be separated; one is simply the absence of the other. This relates only to the physical state: a body lives and breathes and then a body dies. But somewhere in this equation you have to make room for transcendence. The spark of awareness seems to be linked to the body, but is also in some way separate. I have experienced travel without the hindrance of my body. You may say that is a hallucination, but the experience differed in no way from experiences like taking a bus. There were actions and reactions, sensory stimuli – a sensation of being there. In any sense of the word the experience was real simply because it was experienced.

So believing that the mind can exist apart from the body in life means that I have to consider the possibility of the same being true after death. Certainly my apparently real, recent conversations with Greg have forced me to think about it.

If the Church of the Immortals has anything to offer it seems to me that it offers stasis. Remaining alive forever allows for no change in experience. Would you want to be an infant forever? A teenager forever? Why an adult forever? Because death is so bound up with life it has to be part of the process of living and should be embraced as such. Whether it's part of a personal continuum I'm unsure, but that it's part of the process of an evolving life-form is certain. Because death leaves room for birth, new life, new vigour, new ideas, new mutations of the basic pattern. Without death everything remains still. Individuals would survive, but what of the evolution of the human race?

When I can no longer cast a shadow on the world it is my time to make room for another. My path must be the quest for the universal consciousness. In the billions of galaxies life assumes a myriad of forms, millions of strategies for perpetuity, millions of chemical combinations that allow for the support of thought. There is a real possibility that even were we to meet a non-human intelligence, we might not recognize it as such. Our extraterrestrial icons are culturally hidebound. We imagine bipedal beings that organize matter into technological societies because that is what we do. The mushroom experience shows us that intelligence can be supported by biological systems vastly different from the human organism. Haldane's universe is not only stranger than we suppose, but stranger than we can suppose.

I walked to Hartfield's house wondering why I was allowing myself to be drawn into his world. I realized that I had never said 'no' to any of his suggestions. But it was like dipping a toe in the water; I was sampling parts of his world, not committing myself to it. As I walked up Hartfield's drive I counted the cars; they lined the side of his drive and filled his car park. I counted forty-three. A mist hung low on the ground, blurring the outline of trees and deadening sounds. I knocked, and the butler showed me into the ballroom, a huge room that I'd never been in before. It was arranged like a lecture-hall, chairs were placed in rows and faced a rostrum on which stood a lectern. Hartfield came over to me as I walked in.

'Thanks for coming. I think you might find it interesting.'

'I'm sure I will.'

'Sit here.' He put a pamphlet in my hand. 'This'll give you an idea of what this is all about.'

He left me to greet more arrivals and I sat down and read

the pamphlet. Jerry Konstad was going to talk to us about immortality. It was mine for the taking; all I had to do was listen and put preconceptions aside. I looked around at the assembled guests. Every one of them looked prosperous, well-dressed and well-groomed. There was a lot of money in this room. Hartfield walked up to the lectern and welcomed us to his house. He asked White Cloud to say a few words. She spoke in a strong voice, imparting a sense of occasion, a sense of importance to the meeting that we had chosen to attend. She introduced Jerry Konstad, and left him the stage.

He was a small man, five-foot-six maybe, with silver hair and an expensive haircut. His suit was dark grey and well cut; a large and heavy gold bracelet occasionally appeared from beneath his cuff. He had an infectious smile and pearly white teeth with a perfect bite. He spoke slowly at first, looking up very little, but gradually his speech quickened, his movements became darting, he walked the rostrum, his gestures punctuating his staccato sentences. There was a real sense of evangelism in the room, palpable excitement. We were chosen people; we were being offered extraordinary knowledge long hidden from the masses, known only to a few adepts. Wisdom that had been known through the ages, but kept secret. Now, through the Church, we could become privy to something divine – the same immortality enjoyed by the gods. History was being rewritten, the future belonged to those who would be immortal. The choice was ours.

'To succeed in its mission the Church needs your commitment. I won't beat around the bush here; the truth is too important. For our church to bring its message to the whole of the human race we need your whole-hearted commitment. We need to buy air-time, print pamphlets, bring together our members in conventions all around the globe, spread the word. Without you, each and every one of you, none of this is possible. Who here will listen? Who will heed the message? You? You? You? Who will become immortal?

'That's the gift I offer to you today. Not immortality after death, but immortality now. This is no new discovery – from the ancient Egyptian high priest Imhotep to the Count of Saint Germain, there have been immortals. The philosopher's stone was no trick to transmute lead into gold; no, my friends – the alchemists' search, the Holy Grail, the secret of the Templars, was nothing more than the knowledge I offer you today.

'It is no easy path that I offer you. When you commit yourself to the Church of the Immortals it is for life – eternal life. We are your family, your support, your staff if you will, upon which to lean in times of adversity. For there will be hard times ahead; there will be mockery and wilful misunderstanding, there may even be persecution. You may waver, you may harbour doubts, you may want to turn your back on The Way; but we will be here for you. Eternally.

'Today, right now, a door is opened for you. A new path will be offered you, a path that only the chosen tread. Initiates will devote much of the next two years of their lives to the Church, studying, working and spreading the faith. Does that sound like a long time? Think, my friends, two years is but the blink of an eye in eternity.'

The sense of expectation and excitement was by now throbbing through the room. Jerry stood at the rostrum and called for silence. 'Let the meeting begin.' He paused, and let everyone settle down. 'You!', he pointed, 'what's your name?'

'Marianne Lesley.'

'Marianne, step up here beside me and profess with me. That's it, stand there. Marianne, do you want to live forever?'

'Yes.'

'Louder.'

'Yes.'

'Louder!'

'Yes I do!'

'You want to live forever?'

'I do!'

'Do you dare to be immortal?'

'Yes!'

'Then welcome to our Church. May the Way grow within you. May your belief be absolute and know no doubts. May your certainty shine out like a beacon for all to see. Marianne, with faith, immortality is yours!'

Jerry started the applause, and the room shook with it. One by one he worked his way through the gathering, choosing his candidates carefully and professing them in their new faith. Before he had finished, more people were pledging their lives to him. I was frightened; although I believed it was pure theatre, I could feel the strength of the communal will. The gathering had its own momentum, sweeping all waverers along, like a vortex that fed on the crowd, its appetite continually growing. Once again Jerry called for silence.

'There are some among you who have made no commitment today. We feel no anger toward you, no bitterness; but we are disappointed. You have been offered great knowledge; a wonderful gift has been proffered you, and you have not availed of it. Think on this. A chance of enlightenment does not come to you every day. It is rare and precious. Seize the day; take what is offered to you with an open heart. Let the joy of faith and certitude into your lives. I beseech you, join with us, be a part of our movement, take this step on the road to joy, become as us – immortal.'

In the silence that followed there was only an odd cough, a slight movement of chairs. Konstad's eyes scanned the room, selecting those he hadn't convinced, bullying them with his unflinching gaze.

I stood up. 'I want to ask a question.'

'Ask.'

'Your partner, Joe Kay. Was that his real name?'

'Names are unimportant. It's who you are that matters. Your name is just a label for the sum of your experiences.'

'But was his real name Joe Kay?'

'I think I've answered that. Are there any more questions?' His eyes scanned the room.

'You haven't answered it. I want to know. What was his real name?'

'Please sit down, sir, you're disrupting this gathering.'

'Why won't you tell me?'

'If you don't sit down now, I'll have to ask you to leave.'

He nodded to the back of the room and two large men seized me by the arms.

'Tell me his name! Why won't you tell me his name?' I was bundled out of the room and left in the hall. I was shaking, I couldn't stop my hands from trembling. Hartfield came out and closed the door behind him.

'What did you think you were doing in there? I'm surprised at you, behaving like that in my house.'

'I just wanted to know his name. It matters to me.'

'Perhaps you should go. Yelena and White Cloud really wanted this to be a success. Your behaviour hasn't helped.'

'I'm sorry. I hope the meeting goes well. I just wanted to know his real name, that's all.'

'Yeah, I know, OK. Look, I have to go back in; I suggest maybe you should go home now.'

When I got home the trembling had stopped, but I still felt angry. Why had he refused to answer me? Why all that bullshit about names being meaningless? They're not meaningless, they can give you a clue as to who you're talking about. I wanted to know if Joe Kay was Greg, that's all. The possibility had nagged at me for weeks. It was entirely possible; the time-scale fitted.

I sat in my armchair and watched the flames in the hearth lapping round the logs. I half closed my eyes and thought about my last meeting with Greg at the stones. Was death no more than a dream? A change of perspective, just as a sleeping body dreams, a dead body experiences an other-worldly reality. Maybe. I realized that I was re-running Hamlet's soliloquy. Maybe, maybe not. Sleepers awake and tell of their dreams, the dead say nothing. Unless Greg was talking to me. Talking from across a divide that could only be spanned by deliberately splitting the skin of everyday reality. Mushrooms allowed doors to be opened that normally remain firmly shut. Either that was true, or I was quite simply going mad.

Yet it all seemed so real. Greg spoke as he always had, he spoke of things that he always spoke of. A memory brought to life? That was possible too, but somehow I didn't believe it. Some kind of change was happening to me, as though in preparation for a journey. I've often thought about what I'd do if extraterrestrials knocked on my door and said 'come with us', but it occurred to me that expecting them to behave like humans was a bit terra-centric.

I remembered something Greg had said years ago about mushrooms being star-borne. If he was right, then the mushroom reality was a glimpse of an other-worldly reality. Perhaps the invitation had already come in the shape of the mushroom-induced visions; perhaps because their plane of existence was in no way similar to ours that was how the invitation was made. Perhaps this was how contact was made; not in the world of matter, but in the realm of dreams. Maybe I'd just had my invitation. Now I'd have to decide whether or not to accept.

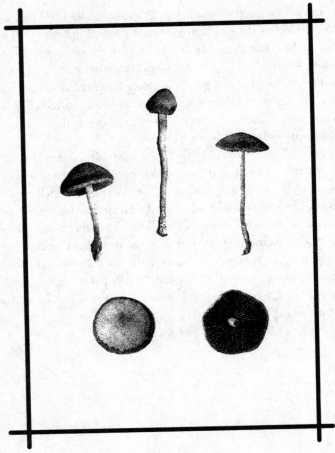

Panaeolina foenisecii.
Small. 1-2 inches high.
Cap dull brown with darker margin.
In lawns and grasslands. Summer to autumn.
Sometimes classified as psilocybin. Hallucinogenic.

fifteen

I felt as though I'd taken one step forwards and now ten backwards. It was deeply depressing. Just as I was confident that I was getting somewhere with the mushroom.man I was back at square one. More obsession with Greg, and not a mention of anything that I'd asked. It was as if he was just sending me e-mail with no reference to what he'd received.

Apart from this sense of going backwards my whole intended schedule was thrown out of gear. I had planned to have my paper ready for reading at a symposium in early November. It was clearly out of the question now. I suppose I sulked. I sent nothing to him and tried to keep my mind on the task of learning the course I was due to teach the next year's intake of students. I stayed away from the net, not checking my mailbox. It was like trying to quit an addiction; but every time the temptation came on me to get onto the net I refrained.

By the end of October I felt I could resume my life on the net, but I was determined to send nothing to the mushroom.man. I felt that he had shut me out by simply not responding to anything that I'd written and sending me anything he felt like, even if it had no bearing on our previous correspondence. When I finally checked my mail-box I found he had sent this, nearly two weeks previously.

Attn. mushroom.seeker.
Subject: magic and death.
13 October.

I think I've been living here, in one place, for far too long.

My physical world has shrunk: the same few people are always there, peripheral to my life. I can't define myself any longer by my interactions with others; there are too few of them to make any sense. The only expanding world I know is the cerebral one.

It's tempting to believe that this is what mystics want to say about attachment to the world. Losing the threads of attachment should be a release of some kind, rather like death. I'm increasingly convinced that consciousness is not a product of the physical body, but rather our consciousness creates an effect on the material universe, and that effect is what we call the body. This makes the movement of consciousness from one state to another easier to deal with. From dreams to altered states to hyperspace to cyberspace to death. All one continuum accessible to the mind, but only one state accessible to the body.

The conversations I've had with Greg since his death have puzzled me. I've seen them at different times as different things, in the hope of making sense of them. I've thought of him as a ghost – a shade from Judaeo-Christian mythology – I've believed him to be a lucid manifestation of my own memory; but now I think I've talked to the disembodied mind – the hyper-dimensional being, the essence that once inhabited the body.

I've been puzzled, too, by the influence of a dead friend. If I were to add up the hours I spent with Greg over the years I'm sure they wouldn't amount to much. Less, possibly, than I spent with Clair. So why should it seem to matter more? I have an answer that satisfies me. It's not a question of how long, but of significance. The things that I did with Greg, the conversations that I had with him, turned out to be significant in my life. He altered the direction of it, changed my priorities, and therefore became significant. I let my destiny become inextricably bound up with his. The closer the bond of destinies, the more intensely linked two lives become. And that's what causes the pain when two destinies become unlinked. When Jane decided to leave for her new life she didn't leave me simply alone, but unlinked. A balloon with its string cut, floating wherever psychic winds blow.

It's not something that we do often, because binding our fates to others carries with it the possibility of emotional pain. When we don't do it, there is no real tie to another person. Clair never really became part of my life and so took nothing from it when she left. And that seems to be true of the few remaining people in my life. I made that bond twice, once with Jane, and once with Greg. Both bonds are broken now, not from my choice, but still they're gone. There is no one I know now that I would start the process with again. I don't want to be exposed and vulnerable any more.

I sometimes wonder what the procedures are that make us either admit or exclude another person from our lives. It can't be just congruence of thought: I could never have stayed so long with Jane if that were the only criterion. We had very different ideas and ultimately different needs, yet for years we twinned our lives. There has to be another plane of existence on which compatibility is founded.

Quite what this other dimension is I'm not sure. There are cultures in the world that believe this other level is the dream state. In dreams we act with and react to people we know in the waking state and also to people we have never met when awake. It's a reality in the sense that it's a manifestation of our consciousness, but it operates by different rules. Maybe at some elemental level we recognize some people as dream-mates. This at least explains why some choices seem so odd in the light of everyday reality and why sexual fantasies often include partners who would seem unlikely candidates in the realms outside of fantasy.

It's possible that the hallucinogenic reality is a place where interactions take place with other people in much the same way as in dreams. Unlike the waking state, these interactions are never verifiable. How do I say to White Cloud or Yelena, 'Did you meet me with a dead friend of mine and have sex with him?' What possible answer could you expect that could make any sense? It's like asking someone you dreamed about do they remember being in your dream. Any answer you get is unlikely to help. It's the old Sufi story of the man who dreamt he was a butterfly. When he awakes he asks himself, 'Am I a man who dreamt I was a butterfly, or a butterfly who is dreaming that it is a man?' Much of the experience in altered states has to remain in that state; you can't take it with you somewhere else. Its validity can only be tested within the framework of its own reality.

We live in many parallel worlds simultaneously, but we are not always aware of the fact that we do. Many people are unaware of their dreams day after day, although they will accept that they must have dreamt. There is also the reality that we sometimes get glimpses of; the one where the thoughts of others for a moment become accessible, where we know who is phoning before we pick up the phone, when we are aware of being watched before we turn around to verify it. These are common manifestations of another reality; one that is accessed easily through hallucinogens, but that breaks through into everyday consciousness from time to time unbidden. The higher levels of awareness that mystics hope to achieve are probably these same realities, arrived at by different means. The point is to make their accessibility biddable, to be able to reach them at will, moving easily from one state to another.

It's fertile ground for the imagination. The arrival of opium into England brought a new vision of reality to the poets and artists. Coleridge and Blake explored the altered state that opium brings and created strange new worlds of the imagination. The dark, brooding gothic landscapes of

Coleridge and De Quincey are clear reflections of opium-induced visions. Byron and Shelley experimented with hashish. This literary pedigree passed through Baudelaire, Havelock Ellis, William James and Aldous Huxley. What binds these disparate artists is their readiness to explore the gnostic world and to exploit its stimulation of the imagination. Despite the best efforts of society to repress attempts at exploring the psyche through drugs, there has been an uninterrupted stream of just that running underground in an unbroken chain from the shamans.

What made governments decide to start a war on drugs was the explosion of LSD in the sixties. Naturally occurring hallucinogens were available only in season and only to those who knew what to look for. They also needed time to gather and to prepare. There is an effort to be made before any use can be made of the harvest. However, a reasonably competent chemist could make millions of doses of LSD in one day. That changes things considerably. Every day is in season, there is no requirement of prior knowledge or time spent gathering. The experience is available to all easily and cheaply, even to those who have no idea what to expect. This is what prompted governments to legislate. As long as psychoactive compounds remained in the hands of artists – people already beyond society's pale – they could be ignored. When they threatened to become mainstream, when proselytes like Timothy Leary popularized them, then it was time for legislation. Today the only political debate about these drugs is how severe the penalties should be for abuse.

Would you ban chain-saws because someone used one as a murder weapon? A tool has no morality, it is neither good nor bad, but morally neutral. The use I choose to make of it defines the morality of my actions, not the tool. It's the same with a consciousness-altering compound. I can use it or abuse it. I make the choice. The point is that because of perceived abuses a useful tool has been proscribed and driven underground. The most obvious and the most direct route to transcendence is illegal.

What sane society would spend vast amounts of tax revenues to build and test the mushroom technology of Fermi and Oppenheimer, while at the same time suppressing the use of psilocybin? The first could be the harbinger of the world's end and yet we refine it; the other could be the point of a new beginning and we attempt to ban it.

Magic is only a parlour trick today. There is no sense of awe in the observer, only admiration for what we know to be no more than prestidigitation. When we see a clever illusion we know it is just that; our personal reality is not under threat. And that is what is so shocking to the initiate of gnosis: the assault on their personal reality. The shaman through his magic and the psychedelic through its chemical structure bend and warp reality creating the same sense of disorientation and wonder. Without the shock of discovery that reality is precarious and nebulous there can be no acceptance that other realities exist.

Today's magicians are a long way from their forebears, the sorcerers. The magic of the sorcerers was not to entertain, but to enlighten. In most tribal societies the sorcerer, witch-doctor or shaman is regarded with a mixture of awe and respect. Mostly they don't live in the village, but are peripheral to it. The world they represent and allow access to is a world apart, and their physical placing within the tribe is a manifestation of that. Their magic is the bending and reshaping of reality.

Shamans access a group reality, a realm of the mind where interactions with others take place unconsciously. In this reality the loves and hates of the group are unspoken. It is the world of desires and needs, the world of forces that drive the interplay of society that we are often aware of but that we rarely explore. It's like a kind of internet with links from and to each individual in the group. In this nexus the psychic tentacles around each mind move about one another in an endless dance, like electrons in a gas. It's a fluid world with no boundaries and no signposts, a world where initiates move easily and quickly and where others either never venture or stumble through haphazardly. This is the place where diseases and love begin. It isn't hard to see the parallels between this and the world of cyberspace, where the shamans are the virus-writers and hackers.

In tribal societies each group member lives in the daily world of harvest or gathering but also in the group mind. The shaman is the policeman of this domain, the place where the movement of minds precedes physical actions. The shaman keeps the peace here, smoothing out hatreds and feuds before they spill over into the physical world. The group feels awe for him because he can also manipulate this world; because he moves so freely and unseen through it he can make events unfold as he wishes, bring ostracism and death, or bring harmony.

The medicine-men of the Amazon start their cure of the sick by bringing the individual's psychic wanderings into harmony with the group cosmos. Diseases are seen as manifestations of inner distress. Behavioural disorders like compulsions are similarly viewed. Instead of focusing on the material world, the emphasis is on the inner world, since the conviction is that the material world is the shadow of the inner. This is diametrically opposed to the view of behavioural psychologists.

In our technological society we have no one to tend the group mind. In the workplace the job is done by the personnel department or by industrial psychologists, but neither of these groups has the cultural place of a shaman, and I would suspect that neither have they the skills nor the understanding of one. The study of group dynamics has become a one-world study. It addresses only the physical and therefore does only half a job. It is often oriented solely toward a goal of greater productivity, and rarely if ever toward a dynamic of group harmony based on inner peace.

If the existence of this world is apparent to you, then you must become your own shaman, since there are none in the phone book. With no guide to bring centuries of knowledge to bear, you make mistakes even when moving cautiously. You must move in the world of the sorcerer and do as he does. He manipulates the physical world by manipulating the inner world. The one casts its shadow on the other.

During the twentieth century we have focused increasingly on the physical world – what we call the real world. All our technology, all our research is firmly rooted in matter. We have chained ourselves to the earth and tell ourselves that it is the pursuit of truth. But scratch a little and still we have a need to soar beyond the ordinary, to transcend. We have separated ourselves from a universe of being without even thinking about it – all that remains is a lingering longing and a partial awareness that something is missing.

What I'm sure of is that the great organized religions of the world were all mystery cults at their inception. Embedded in their core beliefs are the remnants of paths to transcendence that have become with the passing of time no more than the empty enactment of rituals whose original meaning is long lost. Why do Christians take communion and eat their god? On the face of it it's a strange ritual. But to a mushroom-man it makes sense – it's what we do. John Allegro suggested some years ago that mushrooms were at the heart of the Judaic cabala and that many of the Old Testament stories were thinly disguised tales of mushroom cults whose real meaning was clear only to initiates. Whatever was going on at Qumran it was right in the mainstream of gnosis. The language of the scrolls is similar to arcana in other cultures: it is oblique and circumloquacious.

Words and phrases have meanings other than those commonly ascribed to them; parables are multi-levelled, designed to be understood at face value, or at a symbolic level.

Normally we find ourselves able to view the world around us with only one set of criteria. Anthropologists go to the Amazon basin and record the shaman songs. They ask what the words mean, they analyse the melody structure. Yet these songs are designed to be seen, not heard. Under the influence of *ayahuasca* the songs become visual images that hang in the air. Analysis of the lyric and melody are in no way helpful to understanding its purport or design. It's a useful analogy when appraising anthropological information from groups where the hallucinogenic experience forms part of the culture. Things are not always as they seem to the Western mind.

Writers of the ancient world have left us descriptions of the great mysteries such as Eleusis. Since the writers were not initiates their reports are like those of modern anthropologists: they are descriptions of form, not content. In this case objective observation is in no way helpful to understanding what happens. The only way to make sense of it is to participate.

A lot of my half-formed ideas about the mushroom.man now came into focus. There was a rationale behind his chronic use of psychedelics which seemed to be based on his assumption that our perception of reality should be shaken. It wasn't entirely clear to me why it should be so important to him that I should accept that there is more than one reality. It could have been, as I had originally thought, a lonely man with a schizophrenic world view trying to make others see things as he did. Or just possibly it could have some meaning that was escaping me.

I could also see how, in his view of things, there was a correlation between the interconnectedness of people on the internet and his perception of the interconnectedness of tribal groups, but it was hardly a major revelation. His historical perspective on ancient mysteries did make sense to me, especially as he applied it to form and content. But the only thing that really kept me thinking was the idea that 'understanding comes through participation'. It bothered me, probably because it was a thought that was already half-formed in my mind.

I had by now got a long way with my paper and this last message allowed me to complete it reasonably well. I had worked hard to disguise the fact that I had only one field source, drawing wherever I could on quotations from other academics. The mushroom.man had suggested some time back that I read the works of Gordon Wasson, which I found in the university library. My original interest in mushrooms had now become entirely fixated upon the hallucinogenic varieties, although it was still only an academic interest. Wasson's books, especially Soma: Divine Mushroom of Immortality *and* The Road to Eleusis, *written with Albert Hofman, were a revelation. But I had a problem. How could I possibly write authoritatively on something that I'd never experienced? And yet something held me back. Fear, probably.*

Already the picture I'd built up in my mind of the mushroom.man was at odds with what I had previously believed to be true of hallucinogens. My problem was simple: the mushroom.man was, I was sure, someone who was coping with his life as well as anyone else; yet all my firmly held convictions supported the contention that prolonged exposure to hallucinogens was ultimately destructive to both socialized behaviours and thought patterns. I had wanted to prove that he was a schizophrenic, and yet I had nothing concrete to back up the contention. The mushroom.man appeared to exhibit none of the symptoms of schizophrenia other than his belief that reality was unknowable. In truth, his only obsession appeared to be with his past.

I had provisionally entitled my paper 'Chronic Abuse of Psychedelics: its Behavioural and Neurological Effects.' In it I strove to support those ideas that I had held dear, but it was a struggle. A doubt had been implanted and it was growing, Hydra-like, gnawing at my certainties. I wrote and re-wrote my paper — on each revision I added more qualifications, more perhapses, more maybes. Eventually it seemed to express no opinion of any kind.

In a way, my contact with the mushroom.man had put me a little off balance. It was as though my intellectual focus had been pushed in a direction I was not prepared for. I had never intended to become either interested in or involved with psychedelia, yet by degrees that was precisely what had happened. Somehow I had become prey to the contagion of the mushroom.man's ideas. It had all the symptoms of a viral infection; the ideas had infiltrated my mindset and, like viruses, were modifying my existing thought patterns to their own design.

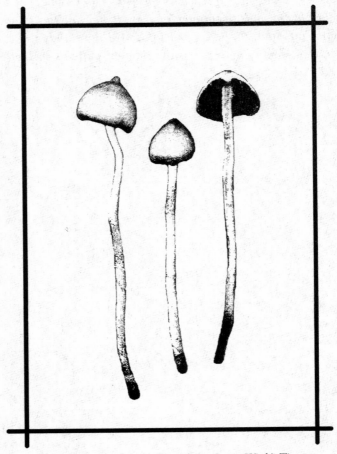

Psilocybe semilanceata. The Liberty Cap or Witch's Tit.
Small. 1-3 inches high. Bell-shaped cap. Distinctive nipple on top.
Cream to pale, darker after rain.
In grasslands especially lawns and golf-courses. Summer to Autumn.
Hallucinogenic.

epilogue

Months passed and I heard nothing more from the mushroom.man. What I had received seemed like the results of a scatter-gun. There was a kind of chronology, but it seemed incomplete. I had a strong sense of unfinished business and became increasingly restless at the lack of response. I tried all manner of rationalizations to explain the silence; holidays, sickness, a broken computer. None seemed to offer a satisfactory explanation. It didn't worry me, however. He'd given me enough to complete my paper and it had been well-received by my peers. I was pretty certain that it broke new ground and was the first of its kind in this area of fieldwork. Other research groups began asking for my opinions or contributions to their papers, which I will admit I found flattering. It looked as though there was a pay-off for the hours I'd spent cajoling the mushroom.man into corresponding with me.

By this time I was fairly sure that I knew where he lived. There were enough clues in what he'd written to know that it was somewhere in the British Isles, although I had already formed the opinion it wasn't England. I also knew a lot more about how the net worked, and by the simple expedient of leaving a message for the webmaster at his on-line address, discovered him to be in Ireland. I began to think about the possibility of visiting him.

It was a thought that hovered for weeks. Endlessly I went over the pros and cons. Did I really want the image that I had built up of him shattered by actual contact? On the other hand, curiosity impelled me to keep considering it as a possibility. Besides, I could rationalize it as a field trip to further my researches. I had more or less decided to go ahead with a visit when an e-mail finally arrived from him.

Attn. mushroom.seeker.
Subject: the usual.
17 December.

I'm sorry to have taken so long to reply to your messages, but a death in the family took me away. I really appreciate the encouragement that you have given me over the months, but with reluctance I feel that our correspondence should end. Since you have shown such regard for my work I offer it to you freely to do whatever you wish with it. I have no further use for it, and no further interest. I'm sorry to be blunt, but my life has taken a new direction and this particular chapter has closed. mushroom.man.

I was shocked at its abruptness. It had seemed to me that we had been building up a rapport which I suppose I had always hoped would end in a meeting. Now he was suggesting no further communication of any kind. It was such a sudden end. That was what finally made up my mind. I would go to Ireland and meet him. I composed my last e-mail to the mushroom.man.

Attn. mushroom.man.
Subject: tapes.
18 December.

Thanks for the e-mail, and thanks for the offer of all your work, it's more than generous. I would like, however, to send you a gift of three tapes of lectures given by Terence McKenna, who I know you know of. Naturally these can only go by snail-mail, so if you'll let me know your postal address, then I'll forward them at once. It's been great corresponding with you. mushroom.seeker.

I flew into Dublin in late January. From the airport a taxi took me to a busy street, a little way from the centre. I was looking for number 42, but hardly any of the shops had numbers on them. While I wandered up and down the street I began to wonder about this address. I had been convinced that the mushroom.man lived an entirely rural existence. This was about as urban as you could get. I walked into a newsagent and asked if they knew where number 42 was.

'Right next door. It's the door next to this one.'

A plain brown door, so nondescript as to be almost invisible, was right behind the open glass door of the shop. Six bells and six names lined the jamb. None of the names meant anything to me; the address I had said simply Flat 4. I picked a bell at random and rang. No reply. Another got the same result. The third brought an old man to the door. He shuffled out in carpet slippers, his hands in the pockets of his cardigan. A cigarette hung from his lips.

'Sorry to disturb you, but I'm looking for Flat 4.'

'Next floor up. Barnes. On the right. American are you?'

'English. On holiday.'

He stood for a while in the doorway of his apartment as I walked up the stairs. I walked slowly, as doubts suddenly began to form in my mind about my visit. It was a kind of intrusion, and may well be ill-received. I faltered, but then I continued. I'd come this far, why stop now? I knocked on the door, hoping that no one would answer it. At least that would give me time to consider what I was doing. I had begun turning away when I heard footsteps inside. I felt a tightening in my stomach. A young woman opened the door.

'Yes?'

'Look, I don't know, maybe I have the wrong address, but I was hoping to meet the mushroom.man.'

'Who?'

'The mushroom.man?'

She stood still and stared at me. I felt nervous and absurd. That primeval urge to flight began to build up in me. Suddenly she smiled.

'Are you the American Adam's been in contact with?'

'That's me.'

'Come on in. Adam'll be surprised, he thinks you're a woman.'

I followed her into a room that was cluttered but tidy. The noise of the buses and traffic outside hung insistently between us.

'You've just arrived, have you?' She pointed to my suitcase.

'Flew in about an hour ago.'

'Sorry, I'm not being very hospitable. Would you like a cup of tea?'

'Please, yes, thank you.'

She switched on an electric kettle and busied herself. I looked around at a shabby apartment. I sat in an armchair that had stuffing coming out of the arms. A spring seemed determined to penetrate the seat of my pants.

She came over with a mug of tea. 'Sorry, I don't know your name.'

'Gregory Armstrong. Most people call me Greg. I'm English actually.'

'God, that's weird. I mean, not your name, just that Greg figures so much. In his writing, you know?'

'I know. And your name is?'

'Sorry, Jane. Jane Barnes.'

'You're not the Jane in Adam's writing, are you?'

'I'm his sister.'

'Yes, of course.'

'Adam's not here. He's gone down to the cottage for a few days. He goes down quite a lot these days.'

'I see.'

We sat in silence while the occasional bus made the sash windows quiver. I decided to let her break the silence when she was ready. After a while she gave a little cough.

'Look, I don't know if Adam will want to meet you. He's a very private person.'

'I'm sorry to have come without warning. Maybe I should go.'

'No, no, that's fine. It's OK. It's just that Adam sort of compartmentalizes things. You know – keeps one set of friends separate from another. He might feel that if he knows you through computers, that well … that that's where he's comfortable. On the computer. Does that make any sense?'

'I think so. I can understand that. Look, I'm staying in a small hotel in Northumberland Road, here's the number. If you're talking to Adam, perhaps you can tell him that I'd love to meet him.'

'Sure. OK. I'll do that.' She got up and moved towards the door. I held out my hand.

'Nice to meet you. Hope we'll meet again.'

'Yeah, I hope so. Nice to meet you too.'

I left the apartment with a strong sense of having leapt before I'd looked. A transatlantic journey for no purpose. I took a taxi to my hotel and unpacked.

For two days I sat watching CNN in my room, waiting for the phone to ring. The only call I had was from my mother, who wanted to know how I was enjoying my holiday. On the third day I decided that waiting in my room for a possible phone call was crazy. I went out to see the sights of Dublin. When I went back that evening there was a message from Adam Barnes. He'd left instructions on how to find him, and suggested we meet the next day at four in the evening. Apparently the cottage was an hour or so outside the city, so I'd need to hire a car.

I slept badly that night. Shallow, restless sleep interrupted by periods of wakening. I kept telling myself that there was nothing to fret about, nothing that should keep my subconscious mind working overtime. Yet the thought that somehow this meeting tomorrow was important in some way kept my mind busy.

I spent the next morning hiring a car and re-familiarizing myself with a stick shift. Driving on the left again did not come easily. I ate lunch in a burger bar and wondered once again if this trip made any sense. On the face of it, it looked insane. I had travelled three thousand miles from what I called home, looking for a man whose only evidence of existence was messages on a computer screen.

Despite these misgivings I couldn't help feeling that I was somehow being adventurous and daring. I was doing something that I had never done before; I was acting impulsively, and I found a very definite frisson of excitement in it. I drank two cups of black coffee with sugar, hoping it would calm my nerves.

By half-past two I could resist no more. I set off on unfamiliar roads in an unfamiliar car. After a while, beyond the city limits, I found myself driving through low hills devoid of houses. Around me were rolling peat bogs, some harvested in strips, with small piles of turf the only evidence of human activity. A low mist hung over the hill-tops. I put on the car's lights as the visibility worsened. It was an eerie landscape; lifeless and brooding. The road twisted and turned through the rolling hills until eventually it began to descend and the mist cleared. Large tracts of forestry lined the sides of the valleys and below me I could make out the occasional shimmer of a river running in winter spate. On the lower ground ahead of me I could see some scattered farm houses.

I drove through a small village that lined the road – a few houses, a church and a few pubs. I was nearly there. I stopped at the side of the road to examine the instructions again. There were no more than five miles to go now, and once again I could feel my stomach knotting. I realized that I had built this meeting up into something momentous and that the chances were that it was likely to be more ordinary than I expected. I turned off the road at the sign for Knockaderry forest and drove downhill along a track lined with cut timber. The track made a sharp turn where a large tract of forestry had been clear-felled and I saw that I was in a valley. A river ran along the valley floor, and I could see, about half a mile away, a clearing and a long, low cottage – a plume of smoke rising from the chimney. I stopped the car and got out.

Not a sound disturbed the air. For a moment I couldn't

even hear bird-song. What I was looking at could have been frozen in time: there was nothing to link this view to the twentieth century. It was as if the colour had been drained from the landscape. A grey, overcast sky and a thin mist left all but the closest trees vague silhouettes. What light filtered through the cloud cover was so refracted that there were no shadows, making everything somehow insubstantial. I got back into the car and drove on slowly down the rutted track.

A whitewashed, slated cottage was the only house on the lane. A neatly kept garden surrounded it. As I stopped the car I could see that the front door was open. The gravel crunched noisily underfoot as I approached the porch, the only sound in an otherwise noiseless valley. I knocked on the door and waited. The silence was intense. I called out, I knocked again. I could see through the open door that a fire was burning brightly inside, casting flickering shadows around the room. I stepped just inside the door and called again. I looked around the room. A sofa was placed in front of the fire, a table lay behind it. One wall was lined with bookshelves, another had a writing desk littered with papers. I noticed a single sheet of paper on the table behind the sofa, held in place by a small pot on one corner.

I walked over to it and read the message 'Eat these.' I took the top off the little pot and saw that it contained mushrooms. On impulse I spun around, only to see the room still empty. I shut the door, picked up the pot and sat down in front of the fire. I held the pot between my knees and closed my eyes. I had a decision to make.

Dusk had begun falling, the room was becoming darker, the firelight more insistent. I lifted the pot and smelt the earthy mushrooms. I thought about turning on a light, but the firelight seemed welcoming and comfortable. I pulled out a small mushroom from the pot and studied it in the fading light. A long, thin stem and a top like a tiny bell. I put it in my mouth and chewed. Maybe I was expecting some kind of instantaneous effect, but as there was no effect at all, I ate another, and then another. The taste was not unpleasant;

earthy and a little gritty, but acceptable. Slowly I ate them all. Without any great thought or deliberation I had eaten my soma and sat back to see where it would lead me.

I twisted my wrist to see my watch by the firelight. Ten past four. I had arrived a little early, but now the mushroom.man was late. I threw a few logs on the fire and made myself comfortable again. I felt what seemed like a cramp in my stomach which slowly gathered in intensity and then with a rush seemed to course upward through my chest and into my brain. For a moment I thought it was some kind of nervous reaction to waiting in a strange place, but then another formed and followed the same course. Then, in an accelerating logarithmic progression, wave upon wave crashed upward and outward, each one tingling my body, exciting the synapses.

I put my head back and stared at the ceiling. The fire was casting extraordinary patterns of lights that moved and melded, changed colour and intensity, exploded and imploded. I listened to the music for a while, enjoying the way the notes altered the pattern of the firelight on the ceiling. I remember that rather casually I wondered where the music might be coming from, but it didn't seem important. I felt no sense of surprise when I saw someone sit down in the armchair alongside the fire. I think that I simply accepted that it must be the mushroom.man and went back to staring at the ceiling. I remember a slight feeling of surprise that I'd never noticed before how music can change patterns of light and shade.

After a while I focused on the armchair. It took a while before the image in front of me resolved into anything coherent. A man with black hair, dressed completely in black, sat there. His face was startlingly clear against the dim background. His eyes seemed enormous; as I stared into them they became like whirlpools of darkness, sucking me into their vortex. I felt a little uncomfortable in his gaze and I tried to go back to watching the ceiling.

'Look at me,' he said.

His voice had an odd timbre. It was brown and gravelly, but deeply sonorous. Only three words, but I sensed a comforting presence from them. When I looked back he was standing, staring down at me. A yellow glow extended all around him for about five inches. While I watched, the glow began to oscillate and move. Slowly the outline changed from that of a man to that of an egg. I could no longer see his legs and the effect was to make him appear to float. I felt the beginnings of a wave of panic. Suddenly I realized that the mushrooms were taking effect, that these strange twistings of reality were beyond my control. I looked around me; wherever I cast my eye it was as though a crystal skin, thin and fragile, covered everything. I felt myself being pulled to my feet.

I heard a voice say 'Come with me'. I made no resistance and followed. Outside the moon was just visible behind a thin layer of cloud, casting enough light to make out the shape of trees and fields. I could see the shape of a man beside me.

'Are you the mushroom.man?'

'Yes.'

'Are you real?'

'The question is, are you?'

There are moments when even the most banal of questions shakes you to the core. I felt my consciousness teetering on the brink of some impossibly deep and dark abyss. I could find no trace of certainty in any thought, no sense of purpose, no centre to my being. It was as if I had suddenly been placed in an infinite void, a place where I had never been, but which somehow was not unexpected. I could feel myself shaking as I tried to find a part of my consciousness that I could get a grip on. Until I could, the question couldn't be answered. Adam's voice was in my ear.

'This is Heisenberg's Uncertainty Principle. In the cosmos of quanta there exist all possible universes. Each and every one is as possible and as probable as any other. Every time you use your consciousness to make a reality of one of them, by definition you exclude the others. It's the choice that's scaring you.'

'You seem real enough.'

'Only because you're hearing my voice.'

He started to sing a strange, sinuous melody. The notes hung in the air between us, as real and as palpable as anything else. They began to form a mosaic, or rather a tapestry. Slowly, as he continued to sing, I began to make out the shape of a mushroom. I reached out to touch it, but my moving hand deformed the image, making it look like a billowing flag. When I took my hand back, the image settled down again. I tried again to touch the mushroom, fascinated by the effect my hand had on the tapestry. It was like shaking a silk screen upon which an image was projected. The song stopped, and at once the mushroom disappeared.

I saw Adam about two hundred yards away, ahead of me on the path. I tried to catch up, but the going was hard in the dark, the path uneven and stony. On either side of it tall spruce and fir were discernible against the sky. Orion's belt was directly above me. I stopped and listened. The trees creaked and groaned in the light breeze. It was a sound that I was not conscious of having heard before. It was the sound of complaint; as though the wind was disturbing their rest. I tried to ascertain how I felt – neither cold nor warm. I rubbed my hands together and was startled by the red glow that the friction caused. My mouth felt dry. I called loudly for Adam and a rush of movement in the trees startled me. A deer jumped onto the path, and in the starlight I could see it clearly, watching me. It was a stag with a massive set of antlers, big, strong, and with a thick russet ruff of winter coat around its shoulders. As I stared at it I began to see that, like Adam, it had an aura-like glow around it. We were both motionless, frozen still in time. I began to experience a strong sense of stag; and how different it felt from my own sense of being. I counted its points – twelve. For a moment it occurred to me that if it charged, those points could do a lot of damage, yet I remained calm. I felt almost god-like in my serenity. I could smell its musk, a strong smell of sex. I remembered that this was the time of the rut. A sudden hand-clap made the stag start and run. Adam came up to me.

'That's the bastard who's destroying my vegetable patch. I'll get him before the season ends. Come on, we've a way to walk yet.'

I found it hard to engage. I had been completely immersed in my communion with the stag. There was a hard-edged cruelty in Adam's tone that disturbed me. I wanted to savour all these experiences without anger, pain or distress. It began to occur to me that although the mushroom experience was different from anything I had ever experienced it was not what I had expected. I was seeing no great display of visual pyrotechnics or trans-sensual stimuli, but finding it to be a more cerebral experience than I was prepared for. I wanted to talk about it.

'Adam, I feel that my mind is in complete control of my body, I mean that everything I feel or want to communicate is under the total control of my mind. Does that make sense?'

'Right now you're in a world of your own creation. Of course you're in control of it, you made it. I can make some sense of what you're saying, but it's probably not what you mean.' He stopped and turned to me. 'There's no way that I can enter your world. The best I can hope for is the assumption that it can't be very different from mine. If it is very different, then there's not much future for communication.'

'I feel really good. I feel like this is the way that I should feel all the time. I like this total awareness of the body. I'm sure that I can see the effects of a force-field all around me. I feel completely in touch with my body.'

'It makes for great sex.'

'I sort of had the impression that sex wasn't a big issue for you.'

'Never believe everything you read.' He burst out into a loud, incongruous guffaw which convulsed his whole body. I could feel the waves of the laugh like a buffeting wind. I began to doubt myself. Perhaps I should never have said what I thought of his sexuality. As I thought upon that, the waves of laughter began to seem hurtful, as though he was laughing at me, not at what I'd said. The waves of laughter kept coming, pushing harder and harder into my belly. I felt I might collapse, like a pricked balloon.

'Adam, stop. It hurts.'

'Keep yourself together. Stop falling apart. It's nothing but self-indulgence. You're a fool if you think you can find truth in the written word.' He gripped my arm. 'Come on, we're not there yet.'

Then I remembered. I had something to tell Adam. Searching the net I had come across a list of poisonous fungi and some case-histories of victims. The name Greg Holder was among them.

'Adam?'

'What?'

'I know how Greg died.'

'What?' He stopped and turned.

'He ate six *amanita phalloides*; death-caps. His autopsy showed catastrophic liver damage from phalloidin poisoning.'

It was hard to concentrate. My mind kept wandering, but I knew that this was information I had to impart.

'There's something else I found out.'

'What's that?'

'Your friend Hartfield Stanley used to run a big software company. He sold out some years ago. Greg used to work for him.'

Adam stared at me. I felt uncomfortable and I had to look away.

'Are you sure of this?'

'I'm not sure of anything right now, but I felt that I should tell you. I found out about it on the net.'

Adam was standing directly in front of me. I looked at his face, lit by the ethereal light of the moon. I became entranced as varying emotions came and went across his face, like a slide show. Once again my mind wandered. Suddenly he spoke.

'So maybe it wasn't suicide.'

'What?'

'Maybe he wanted the mushrooms to take him beyond this life. Into another. I mean, is it suicide if you believe you're just moving from one state to another? Is it?'

He looked at me as though expecting an answer, but there was nothing that I could say. After what seemed an eternity he moved off. We walked through the night, Adam saying little, as though he was saving himself for some special place or appointment that he had prepared for me. Even though the path was uneven and stony, I found that I could put my legs into a kind of auto-pilot that dealt with the business of movement, while my mind was free to wander. In the silence of the night I felt a growing sense of oneness with all that surrounded me. Not just the forest and the undergrowth, but with the stars, with the heavens. For the first time in my life I felt connected to it all; a profound feeling that by being a part of it, all my thoughts and all my actions made a difference. I was not an insignificant nonentity in the enormity of an infinite universe, but a consciousness that could mould and shape the matter of chaos into sense, into comprehension. That was the power of thought.

We were out of the forest and climbing, gently but relentlessly. I felt as though we'd been walking for many hours, even though I felt no tiredness in my legs. I looked at my watch and was surprised to see that it said half-past eleven. Suddenly I began to feel tired.

'Adam, I need a rest.'

'Nearly there. Just over this rise.'

Ahead of us I could clearly see the brow of a hill, lit from behind and below by a silvery light. It had the effect of giving the hill a halo. The last few hundred yards were hard; unyielding, high heather made walking exhausting. At the summit a large, flat granite boulder lay, little mica flecks glinting in the moonlight. As we sat Adam said, 'Look. We can watch the moon set behind that mountain.'

A waxing gibbous moon hung low in the sky. The hills and valleys were bright and clear in the ethereal light. I realized that I'd never watched a moonset. Once again I looked at my watch. Ten to twelve. The setting moon was closing in on the mountain.

'What time does it set?' I asked.

'Just watch.'

My eyes hopped between the moon and my watch. The last speck of the moon disappeared at midnight. I looked at Adam and he smiled.

'Now comes the long, dark night of the soul.' He lay back on the rock and laughed. 'The sun will rise over that hill at twenty-past seven. We'll wait here.'

Stars began to show themselves where the moon had been, their shy light no longer eclipsed by the moon's brightness. I lay back and scanned the night sky. I found the Great Bear and remembered what my old geography teacher had told me about the pointers. I found Polaris and oriented myself. The moon had set in the south-west, to my right. The dawn would be to my left. I turned to Adam, but he had his eyes closed; asleep, I thought.

I was a long way from home, I had no idea where I was, I was tired, cold and uncomfortable. I had followed a complete stranger to the top of a mountain without even asking why. I was a fool, I told myself. A fool to think that this might have a purpose. And then I began to laugh at the absurdity of it. Why should it have a purpose? Nothing else in my life did. And anyway, what sense could I make of anything while my mind was somewhere it had never been before? I lay back and felt my body sink into the rock, as welcoming and as safe as a mattress.

I woke to see the first spidery rays of light breaking over the top of a mountain. A red sky filled the south-east. I felt refreshed and alert. I sat up to watch the dawn, while vague memories of the night formed. Adam. He'd brought me here, Adam the mushroom.man. I called for him: my voice echoed emptily across the valley in the still morning silence. I breathed deeply of the fresh mountain air. I decided to walk towards the stone circle in the distance.